Clash

Fallen Lords MC

Book Six

USA Today Bestselling Author

Winter Travers

Copyright © 2019 Winter Travers
All rights reserved. Without limiting the rights under copyright reserved above, no part of this publication may be reproduction, stored in or introduced into a retrieval system, or transmitted, in any form, or by any means (electronic, mechanical, photocopying, recording, or otherwise) utilization of this work without written permission of both the copyright owner and the above publisher of this book.

This is a work of fiction. Names, characters, places, brands, media and incidents are either the products of the author's imagination or are used fictitiously. The author acknowledges the trademarked status and trademark owners of various products referenced in this work of fiction, which have been used without permission. The publication/use of these trademarks is not authorized, associated with, or sponsored by the trademark owners.

For questions or comments about this book, please contact the author at winter@wintertravers.com

Also by Winter Travers

Devil's Knights Series:
Loving Lo
Finding Cyn
Gravel's Road
Battling Troy
Gambler's Longshot
Keeping Meg
Fighting Demon
Unraveling Fayth

Skid Row Kings Series:
DownShift
PowerShift
BangShift

Fallen Lords MC Series
Nickel
Pipe
Maniac
Wrecker
Boink
Clash
Freak (Coming July 29th)

Powerhouse MA Series
Dropkick My Heart
Love on the Mat
Black Belt in Love
Black Belt Knockout

Nitro Crew Series
Burndown
Holeshot
Redlight
Shutdown (Coming May 29th)

Sweet Love Novellas
Sweet Burn
Five Alarm Donuts

Stand Alone Novellas
Kissing the Bad Boy

Daddin' Ain't Easy
Silas: A Scrooged Christmas
Wanting More
Mama Didn't Raise No Fool (May 9th)

Table of Contents

Chapter 1
Chapter 2
Chapter 3
Chapter 4
Chapter 5
Chapter 6
Chapter 7
Chapter 8
Chapter 9
Chapter 10
Chapter 11
Chapter 12
Chapter 13
Chapter 14
Chapter 15
Chapter 16
Chapter 17
Chapter 18
Chapter 19
Chapter 20
Chapter 21
Chapter 22
Chapter 23
Chapter 24
Chapter 25
Chapter 26
Chapter 27
Chapter 28
Chapter 29
Coming Soon
About the Author
1st Chapter of Burndown

Dedication

I've had a hard couple of months, and it's left me thankful beyond words for the people around me.
My boys are my world and without them all of this is for nothing.
My family is the root of everything I do and I wouldn't be able to do any of this without them.

Nikki Horn. Girl, I swear you get me more than I do. Thanks for understanding my days of silence and then responding to my fifty messages in a row acting like I didn't just ghost on you. You're the real MVP.

Stay sassy, ladies.

Chapter One

Clash

"Uh, anyone else see that?"

I looked up from my beer. "See what?"

Brinks slid onto the barstool next to me. "Just passed Raven in the hallway. She had a pack of matches and one of those red gas cans with her."

"Ha, ha. Funny." That was the last thing I needed right now.

"Brother, I ain't fucking kidding."

"Fucking shit." I sprang up, and the barstool under me skidded backward. "Why the hell didn't you stop here?" I demanded.

Brinks held up his hands. "Not my fucking problem."

That right there was bullshit. "You can tell Wrecker that when Raven blows up the fucking clubhouse and you saw her with the damn matches before." I jogged down the hallway past all of the bedrooms and out the back door.

"I wondered how long it would take for Brinks to rat me out." Raven stood in front of the firepit with her arm extended, emptying the contents of the gas can.

"What in the ever-loving fuck are you doing?"

She shook the empty gas can making sure to get every drop out. "Having a bonfire." She tossed the can on the ground and bent over to pick up the pack of matches.

"Whoa, whoa, whoa." I snagged the matches from her hand. "You really think emptying a can of gas on to…" I looked down in the firepit, and my jaw dropped. "Are those Barbie dolls?"

That was an interesting kindling.

She tried to grab the matches from me, but I dodged her reach. "Uh, yeah. You done being Smokey the Bear and gonna let me have the matches?"

"Hell no." I shoved the matches in my pocket. "You ain't lighting this shit on fire."

"Then you light it on fire," she insisted.

"You have a fucking gallon of gas on this shit, Raven. I light that on fire, you and I are likely to go up in flames with it."

She shrugged and folded her arms across her chest. "Some days, that wouldn't be too bad."

"What in the hell is going on with you?"

"None of your fucking business, bike boy. Just give me back my matches and be on your way."

"Bike boy? Have you reached a whole new level of bitch?"

I was at my wits' end with Raven. She was so pissed off at life, but she didn't want to tell anyone why. Wrecker had given me the abbreviated rundown.

Mom dead.

Foster care.

No family but Wrecker.

Shitty hand, but she wasn't the only one who had been dealt shit cards. To me, it was all about how you chose to play them. Right now, Raven was living on the corner of Poor Me Street and I'm A Bitch.

"And have you reached a whole new level of asshole? Last I heard, guys weren't supposed to call chicks bitches."

"Well, the shoe fucking fits, and damned if you don't put that shit on and lace it up."

"Remind me again why you thought you needed to come out here?" she drawled.

Always just talking in circles when it came to Raven. While the chick was hot as fuck, she would fuck with your head without blinking.

"Trying to prevent you from burning down the clubhouse. Pretty sure Wrecker would shit an actual brick if that happened."

"Wrecker, Wrecker," she mumbled under her breath. "Everything leads back to that asshole." She spun on her heel and plopped down in one of the chairs.

"He is the prez, darlin', and you're staying at the clubhouse."

I knew she had major issues with Wrecker, but none of us really knew what they were.

She sighed and stretched her feet out in front of her. "The gas can was only a quarter of the way full. I know you don't want anything to do with me, but can you just light the damn fire?"

"It really that important to you?" I questioned.

She leaned her head back and looked up at the sky. "I don't have anything that's important to me, Clash."

The weight of her words hung in the air. "I find that hard to believe."

"Also don't have much to believe in either," she said softly. "Light the damn fire and leave me alone, Clash. I promise not to light the clubhouse on fire."

"I'm not leaving you out here by yourself."

She pointed to the other side of the firepit. "Then your ass can sit over there and keep your lips zipped. I came out here and didn't tell anyone because I wanna be alone." She leaned down and grabbed a bottle off the ground. "I'm not sharing my bottle with you either."

"Not drinking," I drawled. At least, I wasn't anymore. Raven was in a mood I had never seen before. Don't get me wrong, she was still being a bitch, but for once, I saw something more than that. "I light this fire and I'm the one in charge of it."

"Whatever. Just light the damn thing."

I pulled the book of matches from my pocket and struck a match against the back of it. The fire sparked to life immediately. The flames rose, and I had to take a step back.

"Thought you said it was only a quarter of the can," I murmured.

"Quarter, half? Not like I had a fucking measuring cup or anything."

The flames died down quickly, and the Barbie dolls on top of the wood melted quickly.

"Do I get to ask why we're burning Barbie dolls?"

She took a swig from the bottle and wiped her mouth with the back of her hand. "Sit your ass down, bike boy, and shut your mouth."

There was the hard-mouthed bitch Raven was so good at being. "I'll take that as a no and make up some weird story why we're burning dolls at midnight."

"You do that," she mumbled.

I shook my head and sat down in the chair opposite of her. I watched as she drank from the bottle and looked up at the sky when she wasn't drinking. The moon reflected off her pitch black hair, and I could make out the curve of her lips as her tongue swooped out to catch the drop of liquor.

"You think you can stop being a creeper, bike boy? If you're just gonna stare at me then you might as well talk."

"You are one of a kind, Raven."

She winked and tipped the bottle toward me. "Right back at ya, Clash. Not a lot of guys would follow another guy around like a puppy dog and call it brotherhood."

I shook my head. This wasn't the first time Raven had said something like this to me. At first, it had pissed me the hell off, but now, I knew her hate and rage wasn't directed at me. Since I was the one who was always around that meant I got the brunt of it. That didn't mean I wasn't a little irritated by it, but I got it.

"You want me to stare at the fucking stars or something?"

"Or something," she murmured.

"You glad Mayra is back?"

"Is she back?" She laughed dryly and reached into her pocket. She pulled out a pack of cigarettes and stuck one in the corner of her mouth. "Can I have those matches you confiscated from me?"

I strolled around the fire, struck a match, and held it up to the cigarette. I tossed it in the fire and sat back down. "I still don't trust you with the matches."

Lord knows what else she might have in mind to light on fire.

The light of the fire flickered off the small hoop in her nose, and she smiled. "You expect so little from me, Clash."

"Or is it I expect a lot and I'm just hoping for a break from the madness?"

"Touché," she chuckled. "Now shut up and let me enjoy the sizzle of plastic melting from the Barbies."

"You got it."

I kicked my feet out, crossed them at the ankles, and slouched down in my chair until my head touched the backrest. If this was how Raven wanted to spend the rest of the night, I wasn't going to argue with her.

This was the most relaxed I had been in months, and I was going to take full advantage of it.

Melting Barbies over a bonfire was more peaceful than you would think.

*

Chapter Two

Raven

"Where were you last night?" Mayra eyed me from where she was seated at the table in the common room.

"Fire." I grabbed a coffee cup out of the cabinet and filled it to the brim with milk.

"Excuse me?" Mayra sat up straight in her chair. "What the hell did you set on fire?"

I rolled my eyes and reached into the back of the pantry. I felt around until my hand connected with the tell-tale crinkle of the double-stuffed Oreo bag. "Barbies and wood."

Raven pulled out the chair next to her, and I plopped down with my milk and cookies.

"As usual, I have so many questions."

"As you should." I peeled back the top of the Oreos and grabbed a stack. I placed them in front of me and stole Mayra's fork off her plate.

"Uh, you know there are clean ones in the drawer, right?"

By now, Mayra should know I just didn't give a fuck about anything. That also included the fact she had used the fork before me. "This will do."

I expertly wedged the tine of my fork into the cream of the Oreo then dunked it into my milk.

"Can we get back to what you were burning last night?"

"I told you." I swirled the Oreo around in the milk and drowned it until the bubbles stopped.

"Where did you get Barbies from? Aren't you a little old for them?"

I waited five more seconds then pulled the cookie from the milk. "It's not like I bought them last week, Mayra. They were from when I was a kid."

"Okay," she drawled. "Then why did you burn them? Wouldn't it have been better to just throw them away."

I crammed the cookie into my mouth and wrapped my lips around the tines to clean them off as I pulled the fork out. "Where's the fun in that?" I mumbled with a mouthful of mushy cookie goodness.

"Are you really eating Oreos for breakfast?"

I stabbed another cookie in the cream then dropped it into the milk. "If I would have known breakfast was going to be an inquisition from you, I would have taken my cookies and milk back to my room."

"Then you wouldn't have seen me."

I shrugged. It wasn't like I saw her much anyway. "I would have caught you later."

Mayra rested her elbows on the table and leaned toward me. "Raven."

I looked up from watching the bubbles. "Yeah?"

"What's going on?"

"I'm waiting for the last breath from this Oreo before I eat it."

23

She rolled her eyes. "That's not what I mean."

"Then what do you mean, Mayra?"

I had woken up ten minutes ago and was eating cookies. That was all I knew at the moment. If she wanted to have some deep talk, she needed to not expect me to actually have something to contribute to it so fucking early in the morning.

"I mean, what are you doing?"

I blinked slowly. "I just *told* you want I'm doing. Killing Oreos and eating their delicious carcasses."

Was I stuttering?

Mayra sighed heavily. "So we're not going to have this talk right now?"

I pulled the cookie from the milk and let it drip. "If you want to have a talk, then talk. I don't know what you're trying to talk about so I can't have the talk unless you tell me what the talk is about." I shoved the cookie into my mouth. "Too soggy," I moaned.

There was a fine line when it came to drowning Oreos, and Mayra had just made me cross it by trying to have a talk without me even knowing what the talk was about.

Now, it's Mayra's turn to blink slowly. "I don't even know what you just said."

"Mayra!"

"Oh," I smiled. "Your badass biker is calling you. Run along." I shooed my hand at her and stabbed another Oreo.

"We're not done with this conversation."

Boink called for Mayra again.

I held up the fork with the Oreo on the end and nodded toward Boink standing by the front door of the clubhouse. "I think Boinkers might disagree with that."

Mayra glared over her shoulder at Boink and held up one finger. "I'm coming."

"You see my warden lately?" I hollered to Boink.

Clash had been absent since I woke up. Normally, he was on my tail before my feet even hit to floor.

"He had an errand he needed to run this morning." Boink nodded toward Freak who was sitting on the couch in front of the TV with a huge bowl of cereal in his hands. "Freak's got you until he gets back."

"Behave," Mayra said softy.

I feigned looking offended and held my hand to my chest. "Are you insinuating that I don't behave, Mayra?"

A smirk spread across her lips. She reached over and rested her hand on my arm. "We both know you don't behave, Raven. I just mean try not to kill Freak before Clash gets back here to keep your ass under control."

"He wished he had control of this ass," I mumbled.

She squeezed my arm and stood up. "We'll continue our discussion later."

I nodded. "I look forward to avoiding that at all costs."

"Lord," she mumbled under her breath. "Later, girl."

Mayra practically ran across the clubhouse and right into Boink's arms. Boink nodded to me, and I flipped him off.

I had to keep these guys on their toes. Swear to God, they all thought they just needed to tip their heads and women would do their bidding.

Not this chick.

No fucking way.

"Do I need to put my running shoes on?" Freak called from the couch.

"You looking for a workout, Freak? I'm sure I could show you a couple of things you ain't never even heard of."

I heard him audibly choke on his cereal.

That was what you got when you tried to one-up me.

I finished the last of my cookies and dropped my cup into the sink. I contemplated putting the Oreos back but knew I would be eating them for lunch so just left them on the counter.

"I actually need to get a crap-ton of work done today, Freak, so you lucked out on warden duty."

"Seriously?"

I rolled my eyes and headed down the hallway to my room. There were horror stories circulating around about me, and that was the way I wanted it to be. If any of these assholes took to heart any of the shit being said then I knew they would stay the hell away.

Most did stay away unless they were forced to be by me.

Boinkers had been my initial warden but when Mayra had decided to tangle with the mafia, he moved to protect her, and somehow, I ended up with Clash.

I rolled my eyes and opened my bedroom door.

Clash was the one I was unsure about.

There were moments when I noticed he had the same attitude I did. *Fuck everything.*

I grabbed my laptop and a pile of folders and notebooks. The one good thing about working online was I could work wherever I wanted as long as I had good Wi-Fi

If I lingered too long in my room, I knew Freak would be at my door, and I didn't want that to happen. My room was the only place that was mine. No one came in here unless I wanted them to. That meant the only person who had been in here was Mayra. Even the rest of the chicks had stayed out. Though Clash had managed to muscle his way into my room before I laid down the rules. He could watch me all he wanted, but once I was in my room, his ass did not come in.

"Yeah, she said she's got a ton of work to do. I'm not sure what I'm supposed to do." Freak was on the phone with, I assumed, either Clash or Wrecker when I walked back into the common.

"You get a free pass, Freakers. That's what that means. I like to keep my crazy shit for Clash." I set my computer on a table close to the TV. "Is that my usual warden on the phone with you?"

"Yeah. He wanted to know if you hogtied me yet."

I smiled sweetly. "Don't spoil my plans for him later, Clash."

I heard Clash's chuckle rumble through the phone.

Freak ended the call with a couple of "yeahs" and "okays." "He said he'll be here in a couple of hours since you're behaving today."

I rolled my eyes and plopped down in the chair in front of my computer. "It depends on your definition of behave, Freak. From my point of view, I've done nothing but behave the whole time I've been here."

"Right," Freak drawled.

"Watch your Dr. Phil and leave me alone, Freaker. Mama needs to make some money today." I logged into my computer and got straight to work.

"What are you doing on there?" he asked after five minutes.

"Working. You should try it sometime." I organized my two notebooks and pulled out the sheet of notes I had started.

"You do the same thing as Cora?"

I looked up from my screen. "Huh?"

"Cora is on the computer all of the time. I think she edits books or some shit like that."

I shook my head and looked back down. "Written word is not my thing, Freak. I'll stick with designing shit."

"Better you than me," he mumbled.

Being a graphic designer was better for me. It was what I loved. Being a freelancer left me wide open to do what I wanted and work with who I wanted. Right now, I was working on a rebranding for a large textile company. They had basically shown me their old logo and asked for something better but had no idea what that would be.

To some people, that might seem like a nightmare, not knowing what the client wanted, but to me, it was absolute heaven. These were the jobs where my creativity came to life.

I got lost in my work and didn't have a worry in the world when I was creating.

*

Clash

"How long has she been working?"

Freak looked over his shoulder at Raven. "Since I got off the phone with you this morning."

Raven's head was down, her eyes pointed at her computer screen, and she had no idea I was even back.

"She eat?"

"Nope."

It was half past one and five hours since I talked to Freak. I hadn't planned on being gone for that long, but with Raven actually behaving herself, it was the perfect time for me to run to see my mom and dad.

"Thanks for keeping an eye on her, brother."

Freak turned off the TV and stood. "No problem. Don't know what the hell you guys are talking about when you say she's hard to keep up with."

I clapped him on the back. "Trust me. What you dealt with today is not the normal."

Freak walked down the hallway shaking his head.

I slowly moved closer to Raven, but she didn't even pay me any attention. She was going to have one hell of a kink in her neck, and I'm sure once she actually took a breath from her computer, she was going to be starving.

"Nose to the grindstone, huh?" I pulled out the chair next to her and sat down.

Raven blinked a few times and turned her head to look at me. "When did you get back?"

"Just now. Actually, a couple of minutes ago. I was talking to Freak, but you didn't even know it."

She leaned back in her chair and raised her arms over her head to stretch. "Surprising I didn't realize you were back. I must be getting used to you looking at me all of the time now."

I shook my head. "You may not have caused any trouble for Freak, but I see you are still sassy as ever."

She looked at her watch. "You were gone for a few hours, Clash. Did you expect a miracle or something?"

"Would have been nice, but no." I ruffled through her papers sitting next to her. "What you got going on here?"

She grabbed the papers and set them on the other side of her computer. "Work."

"What kind of work?" All I had managed to see were rough sketches and scribbles.

"Rebranding. Stuff you wouldn't get."

I sat back in my chair. "I think you might have just insulted me, Raven."

"You're so sharp, Clash. Can't get anything past you."

"You hungry?" I wasn't up for bantering back and forth with her. I had a good morning hanging out with my parents, and I didn't need her to wreck it.

"I could eat." She looked in the kitchen and frowned. "I had left a pack of Oreos in the kitchen, but it looks like they're all gone."

There was an empty blue package lying on the counter with two half-drunk glasses of milk.

"Yeah, you really can't leave food laying around and expect there to be some left when you want it later."

That was something to be learned right away. With up to ten guys in the clubhouse at all times, it was a given that food didn't last long around here.

Raven sighed. "I really don't feel like cooking. I'm in the middle of this. Order a pizza."

"Nah, I'm over pizza. We had it last night."

She looked back down at her computer. "You may have had it last night, but I didn't."

"That's because you grabbed a bottle of booze instead of a slice of pizza."

"Just embracing the biker life," she mumbled.

"Never thought those words would come out of your mouth."

Raven was constantly putting down anything that had to do with the club and the lifestyle.

She grunted but didn't say anything more.

"Chinese instead of pizza?" I suggested.

She shrugged. "That'll do. I want three egg rolls, egg foo young, dumplings, and those sugar coated donuts." Her hands rested on her computer, and she bit her bottom lip between her teeth.

I pulled my phone out and placed the order for all the food she wanted and just doubled it for me. "Twenty minutes."

She nodded. "Good. Now, leave me alone until then. I really do need to get this done today."

"Wow, you really are behaving today."

She flipped me off, but her eyes didn't move off the screen in front of her. "Sit and spin, warden."

And we were back to her calling me that. I almost preferred her calling me biker boy instead. Almost…

"I have plans tomorrow," she said absently.

I tilted my head to the side. "Uh, come again?"

Raven hadn't had any plans since she came into the clubhouse. Suddenly, she had a life and needed to go somewhere?

"My hair is driving me crazy. I'm getting it trimmed, dyed, and then maybe a manicure too if I have enough time."

"No."

She looked up. "Say what?"

"I'm not sitting in a fucking salon for hours while you get shit done to your hair."

She smiled wide. "Oh yes, you are. I mean, you could just let me go alone if you don't want to come with."

Wrecker would fucking kill me if I let Raven go off on her own. The odds of her actually coming back were slim to none.

"You know damn well that's not going to happen. Not after you pissed off The Ultra."

She rolled her eyes. "Not hard to do with those assholes."

They were a bunch of assholes, but Raven was good at pushing people's buttons. "Seriously, can't you just do all of that shit here?"

She shook her head. "No. I wanna try something different and need a pro to do it. At least, the first time."

"What happens after the first time?"

A sly smile spread across her lips. "I watch what they do the first time and then I figure out how to do it myself." She shrugged and closed her laptop. "I want it done the right way, but I'm also not made of money."

I hung my head. "What time?"

"Nine."

"So that means it's going to take all fucking day."

She scrunched up her nose. "Possibly." She stood up and cradled her laptop in her arms. "I'm going in my room to finish this since you can't stop talking to me. Let me know when the food is here."

"You mean I get to come in your room?"

One time, I had gone in Raven's room, and she about had a shit fit.

She looked over her shoulder at me. "No. Knock, warden."

She traipsed down the hallway, and I watched the swing of her hips until she ducked into her room.

"The fucking salon?"

I jumped, startled, and spun around to see Pipe in the kitchen. "What the fuck?" I hollered.

Pipe walked out of the kitchen, a cup in his hand and a shit eating grin on his face. "You were so into Raven, you didn't even notice me walk into the kitchen?"

"My back is to the fucking kitchen, asshole."

"Raven saw me, though." He sat down in the chair she just vacated.

Of course, she fucking had. "Good for her."

"So now, you're headed to the salon to get your hair and nails done tomorrow?"

I rolled my eyes and tossed my phone on the table. "Yeah. Maybe I should ask Nikki if she wants to go and then you can take them."

He shook his head. "That shit ain't going to happen. Besides, Nikki works tomorrow. You're gonna have to try to pawn this shit off onto one of the other guys."

I pointed a finger at Pipe. "Mayra."

Raven would definitely rather go with her friend than me.

"Boink and her just left."

"What?"

"Some trip or something. They'll be back in two days."

Fucking shit. "Of course."

"And before you say Karmen, Wren, or Alice, know that if you get all three of them to go, you are going to have a shit-show on your hands because you're still going to be the one going because Wrecker isn't going to be caught dead in some salon."

"You sure? Maybe he could get his beard trimmed or some shit like that."

Pipe chuckled. "Pretty sure Alice takes care of that shit for him. One of the perks of having an ol' lady."

"That and getting laid on the regular."

Pipe held his cup out to me. "True that, brother."

"So now I'm not only a babysitter, I have to spend all fucking day at the salon."

Pipe shrugged. "Guess that's better than dodging bullets, right?"

It was, but not by much.

"Wrecker needs to figure out what the hell he wants to do with Raven."

I wasn't going to spend the rest of my life following her around while she got her hair done.

"The Ultra, man. Things may seem to be smooth at the time, but we really can't get complacent with these guys."

"I know that, but there has got to be something better we can do with Raven than keep her locked up in the clubhouse."

A knock sounded on the front door.

"Who the fuck is that?" Pipe asked.

I stood up and pulled my wallet out. "Chinese."

I paid the guy at the door and gave him a hefty tip for bringing the shit-ton of food.

"Damn, brother. You should have told me you were ordering us all lunch. I wouldn't have eaten."

I rolled my eyes and started pulling out containers. "This is just for me and a Raven. You or any other of these assholes want some, they are going to have to order their own."

"Brutal," he chuckled.

I grabbed an eggroll and munched on it as I walked down the hallway to Raven's room. I pounded on the door and waited for her to open it. She had some shit music playing that made it hard to believe she could even hear herself thinking in there.

The door swung open, and she stood there with her long hair pulled up into a messy bun on the top of her head. She was now wearing a large, oversized sweatshirt.

"Yeah?"

"You're the one who told me to knock on the door when the food was here."

She pursed her lips. "Sorry, I didn't think it would be here already. I figured you were just coming to bother me since you hadn't seen me all day."

"Nah, babe. It was a nice break this morning. One I thoroughly enjoyed."

"Of course," she mumbled. She planted a hand on my chest and pushed me backward. She pulled her door shut behind her and flounced down the hallway. "Thanks."

"You just apologized and said thank you." I stood there dumbfounded.

"Don't get used to it, warden," she called.

Raven was grabbing all of her food and piling it into her arms when I finally came out of my stupor and headed back to the common room.

"You're not eating out here?"

"God no," she laughed. "I still have about six hours of work left to do, and I can't do it with you guys hanging around."

"I'm slightly offended," Pipe scoffed.

37

"Uh, am I supposed to care?" Raven settled the last container in her arms and moved into the kitchen. "I'm taking this fancy basket," she called.

"What?" I looked at Pipe, and he shrugged.

Raven walked out of the kitchen with her food piled into a basket, two beers in her hand, and a plate tucked under her arm. "Karmen or one of the other chicks probably brought it to try to organize shit in the kitchen, but it works pretty good for a food caddy." She held up the basket. "I should have been a girl scout or some shit like that."

Pipe chuckled. "Yeah, putting your food in a basket is totally girl scout worthy."

Raven stuck her tongue out at him and headed back to her room. "Leave me alone, warden. I promise to stay in my room for the rest of the day," Raven called.

Her door slammed, and I'm sure she locked it as soon as she set down her basket full of Chinese food.

"Still with the warden shit, uh?"

I grabbed a plate and fork from the kitchen. "Yeah."

"You sound thrilled with it."

I set my plate down and loaded it up with food. I set the half-empty container of egg foo young in front of Pipe. "Hate it. Not that she fucking cares."

Pipe grabbed the container and looked in it. "What in the fuck is this shit?"

"Egg foo young, dipshit. Try it."

He wrinkled his nose and set it back down. "Think I'll pass on egg foo of some young guy."

"You're an idiot."

He shrugged and snagged an eggroll. "Whatever you say, warden."

He swiped the egg roll through the sweet and sour sauce and shoved half of it in his mouth.

"Didn't you say you ate already?" I sat down and shoveled a forkful of rice into my mouth.

"Did. But you just offered me some of your egg shit so I figured I could take this."

I moved my plate away from him. "You were wrong."

He shrugged and sat back in his chair.

"Nikki working?" I asked.

He nodded. "Yeah. Gotta pick her up in a couple of hours."

He finished the egg roll and reached for another one.

"Get off my shit." I grabbed everything and moved it all to the other side of the table.

Pipe laughed. "You suck at sharing, brother."

"I was an only child. Fuck yeah, I suck at sharing."

Pipe held up his hands. "I hear you loud and clear. I gotta go work on my bike anyway. Nikki and I were on it the other day and the brakes felt a little soft."

He stood up and made one more reach for my food.

"I will stab you with this fucking fork, asshole."

"Touchy, touchy. I think Raven is rubbing off on you a bit."

I flipped him off.

"See." He shook his finger at me. "That's Raven right there."

"Go fix your bike," I mumbled.

Pipe headed out to the garage, chuckling under his breath.

I set my fork on the plate and sat back.

I was not acting like Raven. If that were the case, I would be holed up in my room right now not talking to anyone.

"Fuck that," I grumbled.

Fuck that, indeed.

*

Chapter Three

Raven

"You like?"

I turned my head to the side then faced the mirror. "Like is not the word I would use."

Michelle sniffled and took a step back. "If you don't li—"

I held up my hand and cut her off. "I fucking love it, bitch. I don't know how the hell you managed to make it look like this, but I am never going to another salon. Ever."

Michelle, the hairstylist I had just met this morning, clasped her hands in front of her and spun a circle. "Thank God," she sang out. "I was terrified you were going to hate it."

I gently shook my head and watched the light reflect off my hair. "I don't know how anyone could hate this."

When I had walked into the salon, I had an idea of what I wanted, but Michelle had taken my idea and ran with it. My roots were still pitch black but about four inches down, my hair ombred into a dark maroon color then to bright, fire engine red ends.

It was fucking amazing.

I fluffed my hair with my fingers and smiled wide. "Just the kind of change I was looking for."

"Should we wake up Warden and show him?"

I stifled my laugh at Michelle calling Clash, Warden.

When we had walked in, Clash hadn't been on his toes so when Michelle asked him his name, I was able to sneak in and say Warden. I managed to keep a straight face, and Michelle had completely bought that being his name.

Now good ol' Warden was sleeping in the corner of the salon in one of the chairs that wasn't being used by customers.

"I still say we should have frosted his tips."

Michelle wrinkled her nose. "Girl, that is so nineties." She whipped the cape off and draped it over the chair next to me. "You're good to go."

I looked down at my nails and smiled. It had been months since I had them done. They were now painted pitch black with lace overlay on two of them. "You are a goddess when it comes to nails and hair."

I followed Michelle over to the front desk and kept my eye on Clash who was still sleeping away.

"Thanks for the tip, girl."

I winked at Michelle and shoved my wallet back into my purse. "You earned it." I had taken up most of her day, and she had been pretty cool to talk to. "I better go wake up sleeping beauty since he's my ride."

"He's gonna be shocked when you wake him up."

I rolled my eyes and headed over to Clash. He wasn't going to care what I looked like.

His feet were sprawled out in front of him, and his legs were cocked open. His head was tipped back, and his mouth was hanging open.

"So sexy," I whispered.

I kicked his boot, and he sprang up out of the chair.

"What the hell?" he shouted. He looked around frantically until his eyes landed on me.

"Easy, warden. You were taking a little *siesta* there."

He wiped his mouth with the back of his hand. "No, I wasn't."

I rolled my eyes and hitched my purse up on my shoulder. "Right. You were just trying to catch flies."

"You done?"

I waved my nails in his face. "All girlied up."

He grabbed my hand and held it still in front of him. "Nice. Black and lace. It's oddly fitting for you."

I yanked my hand out of his grasp. "How nice of you to notice."

His hand reached up, and he wound a strand of hair around his finger. "This is what you had up your sleeve?"

He studied the strand of hair, and an odd sensation washed over me. I was worried he wasn't going to like it.

What the hell?

Since when did I care what Clash thought about me? Let alone anyone for that matter?

"Yeah, it's what I wanted. You got a problem with that?"

He dropped the hair and took a step back. He looked me over, and I fidgeted under his gaze.

"Let's motor, warden. I'm starving."

43

He grabbed my hand and pulled me close. "Not so fast."

"What are you doing?"

"Give me a second to wake up, woman."

I huffed and rolled my eyes. "Wait until I tell Wrecker you slept on the job today."

"He's already impressed that I even came with you today. I doubt he would care I fell asleep." His thumb gently grazed over my wrist. "Your hair is unlike anything I've ever seen before."

"Then you really haven't been paying attention to anything. At least, not chick's hair."

He shook his head. "Yeah, gotta say, I'm not really looking at girl's hair all of the time." His eyes connected with mine. "Seems to be you're the only chick I notice these days."

"Only because you don't want me to light the clubhouse on fire."

"Yeah," he chuckled. "That's got something to do with it."

I looked over his shoulder and tried not to think about the way it felt when he touched me. "I'm starving. My stomach is literally trying to eat itself right now."

My stomach had actually dropped to my feet, and I was trying frantically to figure out what in the hell was going on. It was like Clash had fallen asleep and then woken up like he had never seen me before.

He let go of my arm and dropped his hand to his side. "Then let's get you fed."

Clash ushered me out of the salon, his hand resting on the small of my back as we walked past Michelle who was still at the front counter.

And then I remembered we had driven Clash's motorcycle here and I was going to have to wrap my legs around him.

Shit.

I had ridden on the back of his bike before. Hell, that was how we had got here, but now, it felt different.

I was feeling different, and I had no idea why.

"What are you hungry for?" Clash handed me my helmet and stood watch while I strapped it on.

"Uh, pasta?" Why? Why in the hell had I said pasta? I should have said I changed my mind and that I wanted to go back to the clubhouse. Instead, I said pasta which meant we weren't going to be able to eat quickly. "Or hot dogs."

Shoot me now.

Clash tilted his head to the side. "Pasta or hot dogs? What in the hell happened in that salon while I was sleeping?" he chuckled.

I was afraid the hair dye was going to my head. "Or we can go back to the clubhouse and see what there is to eat there. I'm sure by the time we get back, one of the other chicks will already be cooking."

"But what if they're not cooking hot dogs or pasta?"

45

I rolled my eyes. "You're an ass. Take me back to the clubhouse."

There was my inner bitch coming out. If she had waited any longer to come out, Clash really would have wondered what the hell was going on.

"Hold on, now. I like the idea of pasta. Nickel was telling me about a new place that opened a month ago." He pulled out his phone and typed something out. His phone dinged instantly. "Café Tella. That's where we are going for dinner."

"I'd rather go home," I insisted.

Clash shook his head and shoved his phone back in his pocket. "And I want pasta now since you are the one who brought it up."

"Forget I ever said it. Just take me back to the clubhouse and forget I ever said anything."

"Not gonna happen, babe." He threw his leg over his bike and looked over at me. "Get your ass on the bike."

"What if I don't?"

"Then, I'll *make* you get your ass on the bike, and I really don't think you want that to happen."

I folded my arms over my chest. "Try me," I challenged.

Damn right, I was going to call his bluff. Clash was talking a big game, and I didn't think he would actually do it.

"We really gonna do this?"

"I don't know, are we?" I countered.

Clash shook his head and swung off the bike. He had me in his arms before I could even move an inch.

"Hey," I protested. "You didn't even give me a chance to move."

"Not here to give you a chance, babe. I'm here to keep you safe."

His arms were wrapped around me, and I was pulled flush against his chest.

"Uh. What just happened?"

"You said you were hungry and then all of a sudden you want to go back to the clubhouse to scrounge for whatever is there. I wanna know what just happened too."

I put my hands on his chest and tried to push away from him. He didn't give me an inch.

"I'm talking I want to know how I'm here." I looked down at my hands on his chest. "With you."

"New strategy."

"Strategy?" I parroted.

"Yeah."

"Am I supposed to know what that means?"

He shook his head. "Nope."

I blinked twice and tried to process what he just said. "Is this your new strategy to deal with me?"

He smiled but didn't speak.

"This is a sure fire strategy that is going to lead to me kneeing you in the nuts." I just had to take half a step back and my knee would connect directly with his nuts.

"Not the strategy I had in mind," he drawled.

"Well, whatever strategy you think you have, you can just kiss it goodbye."

"Kiss it?" he said quietly. His eyes warmed, and the corner of his mouth hitched up. "You just told me to kiss it?"

"Your strategy, Clash. Strategy," I clarified.

"That's it? That's all I get to kiss?"

Lord have mercy. His hand tightened around my waist, and he bent down 'til he was a breath away.

"Clash," I gasped.

"We're going out to eat and then I'm taking you back to the clubhouse." His voice was low and stern. "I just sat for seven hours in some froufrou salon while you got even more pretty, so I think I deserve some fucking food that is better than whatever you can scrounge up at the clubhouse."

"Oh, uh, okay," I stuttered. "I, uh, guess that's okay."

His lips hovered above mine, and for a second, I thought he was going to close the gap between us. "Thought you would see it my way." He winked lazily and took a step back. "Get your ass on the bike, beautiful."

I watched as he threw his leg back over the bike and started it. He revved the engine and glanced over at me.

He didn't have to say anything.

I needed to get my ass on that bike because if I didn't, I was pretty sure he was going to kiss me until I did.

*

Chapter Four

Clash

"Leave it."

"No."

"It's not going to fit on the bike."

Raven rolled her eyes. "I'm not leaving all of this food here just to be thrown away. That's wasteful, Clash."

"Woman, we are riding a damn motorcycle. We don't have a backseat where we can set that on the way home."

Raven scraped the last of her food into the container and snapped the lid shut. "I'll make it work."

I didn't know how the hell she was going to make that work. "Is it your mission in life to disagree with whatever is said to you even if you're wrong?"

She rolled her eyes and made a reach for the check.

Another fucking thing she was arguing with me about. I grabbed the little black folder with the bill and laid it in my lap. "You're not buying me dinner."

"You drove," she insisted.

I slapped a fifty inside the thing and tossed it on the table. "Let's go."

She huffed but got up without freaking out on me.

Now we had to figure out how we were going to get to the clubhouse on the back of my bike with a Styrofoam container of lasagna.

The sun was half set, and there was a light breeze when we walked outside.

"So, how are we going to do this, babe?"

"Get on the bike, and I'll take care of the rest."

"You really think I'm going to go for that?"

She had chilled once we got to the restaurant, but I was always on edge when it came to Raven. I never knew what she was thinking or planning.

When she woke me up at the salon, I didn't know who the hell I was looking at for a second. Her normal pitch-black hair was laying in waves around her face, and the ends tapered off to a bright red. It wasn't anything I ever thought to do someone's hair, but damned if Raven didn't pull it off and make it look damn good.

I still didn't know what the hell happened when we were deciding on where to eat. First, she basically demanded to go out to eat, and then suddenly, everything changed and she just wanted to go home.

When she flipped, I had pulled the plan of action out of my ass because I saw an opening I had never seen before.

Raven had looked at me like I was more than a piece of shit on the bottom of her shoe. And damned if she didn't make me feel shit for her that I hadn't felt for anyone in a long damn time.

I wasn't about to let her know that, though. She would use that against me in a heartbeat. Though she did seem completely thrown off her game when I said I was going to kiss her.

"I get on the bike and you take off like a shot?"

She rolled her eyes. "No. Here's why you know I won't do that. I have nowhere to go, Clash. I'm in a town where I know absolutely no one but you and everyone in the club." She huffed and cocked her hip out. "Get on the bike and take me back to the clubhouse."

I threw my leg on the bike and was surprised as hell that I felt the warmth of her body pressed up against me before I even started the bike.

"What the hell?"

Raven's arms wrapped around me, the Styrofoam container knocked my forearm, and then she set the thing on my crotch. "Drive."

"How the hell am I supposed to drive with that thing on my dick?" I demanded.

This shit was not going to work for me.

"Children in Africa are starving, Clash. We are not leaving this lasagna for the mice to eat."

I glanced over my shoulder. "You did not just pull the mom card on me about starving children."

"I did. Now drive." Her arms tightened around me.

I looked down and saw her manicured nails gripping the container of food. Her hands that were within inches of my dick. I guess I was okay with this.

I cranked over the bike and headed back to the clubhouse.

The ride was quick, and thankfully, the container of food didn't catch the wind and plaster lasagna all over me.

Raven scrambled off the bike, the container in her hands, and beelined into the clubhouse.

"She couldn't get away from you fast enough." Wrecker was sitting on the old wooden bench by the front door with a cigarette hanging out of his mouth.

I knocked the kickstand down and killed the engine. "And that's surprising to you?" I drawled.

"Nah, what's surprising to me is you actually let her bring that container back with you."

I growled and rose off the bike. "Trust me. I didn't let that happen without arguing."

Though, I didn't really put up that much of a fight.

"But I see she still won."

I sat down next to Wrecker and sprawled my legs out in front of me. "It's about fifty/fifty of who wins lately."

"Those are pretty good odds when it comes to Raven."

They were. A hell of a lot better compared to when I first started keeping an eye on her.

"So what's going on?"

Wrecker reached to the side of the bench and grabbed a half empty bottle of whiskey. "Alice called a meeting of the Girl Gang."

"So they're all in there getting drunk and figuring out ways to make our lives more crazy."

Wrecker nodded. "That is exactly what they are doing. I'm sure they'll try to wrangle Raven into it too, so just be aware."

I shook my head. "I really don't see Raven falling in with the ol' ladies. You and I both know she bucks anything that has to do with the club. Alice and the rest of the girls included."

Wrecker took a slug off the bottle. "Right, brother. You really don't know the resistance and power of those chicks when they all get together and agree on something."

"And you're doubting Raven's bitch factor."

"Watch yourself," he growled.

I turned to look at him. "Pretty sure I get to say that since I've spent more time with your sister than you have in the past ten years."

"You really wanna discuss Raven with me as if you really care about her?"

No one discussed Raven with Wrecker. We all knew the bare minimum and that was bullshit since I was the one who had to be with her twenty-four seven.

"Don't see why I wouldn't care about her."

"Because she's a fucking task for you, Clash."

She had been to begin with, but I wasn't so sure about that anymore. There were reasons why she acted the way she did, and I was interested as fuck to know why.

"I can't take an interest in the things I'm doing for the club?"

"What you need to be interested in is Raven not setting the fucking club on fire."

I shook my head. "Fucking Brinks has a big mouth, I see."

Wrecker shook her head. "I saw her headed out that way. I figured you wouldn't be too far behind."

"Any reason why *you* didn't follow her out?"

A smirk spread across Wrecker's lips. "'Cause it ain't my fucking job to keep an eye on her."

"She's your fucking sister. You really think it would hurt for you to take a little bit of interest in her?"

"You sitting here trying to tell me what to do?"

This is where things could get real fucking hairy with Wrecker if I wasn't careful with my words.

"Not what I meant. Just saying, she is your sister."

"Thanks for the newsflash, dickhead." Wrecker dropped the butt of his cigarette in the dirt and ground it out with the heel of his boot. "Now, why don't you do your fucking job and keep an eye on my sister."

"Is that how that goes?"

Wrecker stood up and looked down at me. "That's exactly how it fucking goes."

He turned on his heel and stormed back into the clubhouse.

That was fucking great.

I didn't want to piss off Wrecker, but I was fucking sick of knowing nothing about what was going on with Raven when I was supposed to keep an eye on her.

I was just trying to get a better grip on things. Instead, I pissed Wrecker off and was just as clueless as before.

Obviously, Wrecker was not going to be the way for me to get more information on Raven.

*

Chapter Five

Raven

"Where?"

"Hair Barn. Michelle did it."

Alice picked up strand of my hair and inspected it. "I think Michelle and I are going to have to get acquainted."

"Make sure you take Wrecker's wallet with you," Karmen snickered.

That was the damn truth. Michelle had done an amazing job, but she had definitely put a dent in the advance from my latest client.

"You shouldn't make him go with you though," I laughed.

It was a miracle Clash had gone with me. I didn't think there was a chance in hell that Wrecker would go with Alice.

"Oh, hell no," Alice laughed. "He'd ask her up front how much it was going to be, and we would be out the door before I plant my butt in the chair."

"Where you planting your ass, woman?" Wrecker walked into the clubhouse, and I was surprised Clash wasn't with him.

"Did you see Raven's hair?" she chirped. "I'm thinking my purple could use a bit of a refresh."

"Your hair looks fine." Wrecker moved behind the bar and set up a few of glasses. "Or have one of the other chicks do it for you."

"My chicks aren't hairdressers," Alice retorted.

Wrecker filled the three glasses half full with whiskey then filled them the rest of the way with Coke. Those were going to be some strong fucking drinks.

"Not my problem," he mumbled.

"Just give her your credit card," Nikki called. "You know you want Alice looking hot."

Wrecker grabbed the drinks and moved to the table Pipe and Nickel were sitting at. "She always looks hot. Try again." He handed them each a glass then sat down. "Clash is outside. Deal him in."

Nickel dealt out the playing cards and then took a drink. "That'll put hair on your nuts," he chuckled.

"How are you going to play cards when we're trying to have a meeting?" Alice called.

Wrecker turned in his chair to look at her. "Woman. Didn't I make a room in the back for all of your crazy shit? You are not kicking me out of my common room so you guys can discuss hair and whatever the fuck else."

Alice scoffed. "We discuss *way* more than that," she insisted.

"Yeah," Nikki hiccupped. "Last time we got together, Mayra told us everything that happened."

"What?" Wrecker growled.

"Shh," Alice hushed Nikki. She motioned for her to zip her lips.

Nikki's eyes bugged out, and she realized she had just spilled the beans. "I mean, we totally only talk about hair."

Wrecker turned back around and shook his head. "Ol' ladies are going to be the fucking death of me."

Alice plopped down on the couch next to Nikki. "If you would just clue us in when something is going on, you wouldn't have anything to worry about," she advised Wrecker.

The front door opened, and Clash walked in with a half empty bottle of whiskey dangling from his fingertips.

"'Bout time you got your ass in here," Wrecker mumbled as he picked up his cards and looked them over. "Nickel dealt you in."

"You guys were getting Raven's hair done this whole time?" Karmen asked.

I walked around the bar and grabbed a bottle of beer from the fridge. If everyone else was going to drink, I didn't want to be left out. "No."

"Went out to eat." Clash sat at the table with the guys and slammed the bottle down.

"I got leftovers if anyone wants them." I lifted the lid of the container, and the smell of the lasagna wafted out.

"You brought leftovers home?" Karmen asked. "How the heck did you manage that? Nickel always tells me I can't bring my leftovers home if we are on the bike."

I smiled wide. "Clash told me the same thing. I didn't listen."

"Imagine that," Wrecker mumbled.

Alice walked over to the open container. "Oh, my God. Is that Café Tella?"

I nodded.

"Karmen," Alice called. "Get forks and plates. Nikki, meeting has been moved to the bar."

Nikki grumbled but rolled off the couch and hauled her ass over to the bar. "This better be worth it," she grumbled.

"I only got forks cause I'm not interested in doing more than these for dishes." Karmen set the forks next to the container of food and sat down at the bar.

Alice dug into the lasagna and closed her eyes as she moaned. "Sweet heaven above, that is some good shit."

Karmen shoveled in a mouthful, and she also closed her eyes. "Good God."

It had been damn good. Way better than any lasagna I could make.

"You check on Cole lately?" Nickel called.

"I did," Karmen called around a mouthful of lasagna. "But I will remember the next time you're in one of your meetings for the Fallen Lords to interrupt and ask you the last time you checked on Cole."

Nickel looked up from his cards. "You shitting me right now?" he chuckled.

Karmen shrugged and licked her finger. "I guess you'll just have to wait and find out."

Pipe chuckled. "Looks like you'll be the one checking on Cole next."

Nickel flipped him off but didn't disagree.

These chicks were a lot tougher than I had thought they were.

"We should all go out one night," Alice mumbled. "Get dinner or go bowling."

"Bowling?" Nickel chuckled.

Alice grabbed my beer and took a drink. "Sure. Why the hell not? You guys too cool to bowl or something?"

Nickel shook his head. "I'm not. But I'm pretty sure I would pay good money to see Wrecker put some ugly fucking shoes and throw a ball down the alley."

Wrecker shook his head. "Find a bowling alley with a bar and that is where you will find me. My ass is not bowling."

"That's what he thinks," Alice whispered.

"What was that, woman?" Wrecker called.

"Nothing, snookum," she replied sweetly.

Nikki raised her hand. "I would like to request a blue ball."

"You're cut off," Pipe called.

"What?" Nikki shouted. "I am not cut off."

"You just want a blue ball so you can tell everyone you have blue balls or something crazy like that."

Nikki lifted her glass to her lips. "He knows me so well." She took a long drink and winked at me.

Something was happening.

I was being accepted into this weird Girl Gang. "I'm heading to bed."

I didn't want this. I didn't want to be a part of this.

I was supposed to hate all of this and all of them.

Not planned bowling nights and being a part of their meetings.

"No, you're not." This came from Clash.

"Yeah, I am," I insisted.

"Keep your ass behind the bar," he growled.

"No."

Clash took a pull off the bottle of whiskey. "Yes. I can see you and know you're not trying to start the clubhouse on fire."

"I'm not going to set the clubhouse on fire."

One time I go outside with a gas can and matches to light a fire and I'm forever known as setting the clubhouse on fire.

"You stay behind that bar and I'll know that for a fact."

I rolled my eyes. That was the last thing I was going to do. "Deal me in."

"Uh, what?" Alice croaked.

I walked around the bar and pulled out the chair next to Clash. "Deal me in. If you want me to stay out here, then

I'm going to do what I want. Deal. Me. In." I enunciated each word slowly.

"Boom," Alice whispered loudly.

"Can she do that?" Karmen hissed.

"I don't know, but I'm totally popping some popcorn." Nikki dashed into the kitchen with her drink sloshing onto the floor.

"You're not playing, Raven." Wrecker picked up his cards. "We already dealt."

I sat back and crossed my arms over my chest. "I can wait until the next hand. Clash is going to win this one anyway because he has full house, kings high."

Pipe threw his cards up in the air, and Wrecker and Nickel threw them on the table.

"What the fuck?" Clash yelled. "You could have at least waited until they made their bets."

I rolled my eyes and reached to grab the discarded cards. "What would have been the fun in that?"

"It would have put twenty bucks in my pocket. That sounds fucking fun to me." Clash tossed his cards in front of me. He grabbed the bottle of whiskey and took a long swig.

"So now instead of taking it from you, I'll take it from these guys." I shuffled the cards and dealt out five to each of us. "Let's see how lucky you biker boys are."

"Don't start without me," Nikki called from the kitchen.

"It's not like you're playing," Pipe called.

"I know." The microwave slammed, and Nikki came jogging out of the kitchen tossing the hot bag back and forth between her hands. "I want to watch Raven kick your ass."

Pipe looked up from his cards. "Who the hell's side are you on, woman?"

Nikki sat at the bar with Karmen. "Raven's. You're the one who is intruding on a Girl Gang meeting, so it's only fitting you would get your ass beat by her."

"You guys started without us?" Wren walked through the front door with Maniac in tow.

"Hey, I thought I was the fifth guy." Maniac stopped in his tracks and stared at me sitting in his chair.

"I thought we were having a meeting?" Wren pulled a notepad out of her pocket. "I even brought this to take notes."

"Notes?" Wrecker asked.

Alice jumped up and pointed her finger at Wrecker. "See! Our meetings are way more official than yours because we take *notes*."

"Is that cow print?" My mind registered what Alice was wearing.

Cow print overalls.

She looked like a farmer who had decided to skin one of his cows and wear it as pants.

They were absolutely hideous.

Alice hooked her thumbs through the suspenders. "Sure are. You like them? I got them off eBay."

"Ask her how much they cost," Wrecker grumbled.

"They were a birthday present from you," she whined at Wrecker.

"That I didn't know I bought you until I saw my credit card bill." Wrecker leaned back in his chair. "Had to figure out what 'men's jogger cow overalls' were when I looked at the bill."

"It's pretty self-explanatory to me," Nikki laughed. She pointed at Alice. "They're that."

"Alice was kind enough to point that out to me when I asked her what the seventy-nine dollar charge was." Wrecker stroked his beard and laid down one card.

"You paid seventy-nine dollars for that thing?" I asked. I handed Wrecker another card and tried to focus on my own hand and not Alice's pants.

"It was actually a steal. I was bidding on another pair that went over one hundred." Alice spun in a circle and raised her hand over her head. "Wrecker doesn't recognize I got one hell of a deal."

Each of the guys asked for cards, and I set down two.

"She acts like I got off easy or something." Wrecker placed his bet. "She's failing to mention the three Mary fucking Moo Moo statues and the tail."

"Tail?" Karmen yelled. "What in the hell do you need a tail for?"

Alice rolled her eyes and trounced behind the bar. "You really need to tell the whole tail story, and not that I just ordered a tail. You make me sound crazier than I really am."

She grabbed a glass and slammed it on the bar. "*You* are the reason I needed a new tail in the first place."

Nikki leaned closer to Karmen. "You think they're into mascots?"

Karmen wrinkled her nose. "I really don't know what you are talking about, but I am completely intrigued."

"Don't, Nikki," Pipe warned. "Do not open this can of worms."

Nikki rolled her eyes and flipped off Pipe. "I'm totally opening it, Pipe. This needs to be known. People dressed up as animals and fucking is not something that needs to be known."

Nikki slammed her hand down on the bar. "And now you ruined the shock value."

Pipe rolled his eyes and turned around to look at Nikki. "You told the damn cashier at Burger King the other day about mascot fucking. Can we find something else to focus on?"

"I'm not into that," Alice called. "I just like, well, cows."

"I can vouch for the fact that we do not fuck dressed up as mascots." Wrecker looked at Alice. "At least, not yet."

I wrinkled my nose and laid down my cards. "Can we please not talk about this."

Wrecker was my brother, after all, and I did not need to know any of this about him. My hand was shit, and if we kept talking about Wrecker and Alice, I was going to lose my dinner all over the table.

The guys laid down their cards, and Clash grinned wide. "Remind me again how you were going to take all of our money."

I took a drink and glanced at Clash. "That was luck." I grabbed all of the cards and reshuffled them. "Now you really better hold onto your wallets."

I dealt out another hand and breathed a sigh of relief when I saw I had a full house with jacks high. Not the absolute best hand, but I was pretty sure I could win with it.

Wren raised her hand. "Can we get back to why Alice bought a tail?"

Wren was normally the quiet one of the group, but when she talked, she always had a good point.

I, too, wanted to know why the hell Alice bought a tail. "I'm going to need the answer to that, too." I passed on picking up cards and bet five dollars. Clash tried to look at my hand but I lifted my shoulder and glared at him. "Keep your eyes to yourself, warden."

He smirked and leaned back in his chair. "I'll pass."

He bet five dollars, and I wondered just what cards he had to make him think he could beat me.

"Wrecker pulled mine off."

Everyone stopped talking and looked at the kitchen.

Alice had the gallon of milk in her hand and the cap to it in the other.

Nikki elbowed Karmen in the ribs. "They're into mascots but they don't know that's what it's called."

"We are not into fucking like cows," Wrecker thundered.

Karmen leaned closed to Nikki. "The fact he is so defensive about it makes me think you're right."

Nikki nodded and tapped her finger to her nose. "Right on, girlfriend." Nikki turned to Wren. "Are you taking notes?"

Wren had her nose buried in the notepad. "Uh, yeah. You can't even make this shit up. We need to have this all documented."

"Lord, girls." Alice poured a glass of milk then spun the top back on. "I was wearing my pajamas with the tail, and Wrecker was laying on it."

"It just gets kinkier," Nikki hissed.

Alice laughed and shook her head. "Hardly kinky."

She set the milk in the fridge and walked back over to the bar. She popped open a Coke and poured it into the milk.

Nickel curled his lip. "What in the hell are you drinking?"

Alice smiled. "It tastes like a melted Coke float."

"The tail!" Wren shouted. Her pen was poised over the notebook, and she was glaring at Alice. "What happened to the tail?!"

"I rolled over, and the damn tail stayed under Wrecker."

Nikki's jaw dropped.

Karmen closed her eyes.

Wren dropped her pen. "Are you shitting me? That is the ending you're going to give me? You couldn't even spice it up a bit?"

Alice shrugged. "So, I ordered a new one off eBay when I snagged these fancy overalls." Wren glared at Alice. "It was on sale? That has to make the ending good, right?"

Wren ripped out the page she had been scribbling on and tossed it on the floor. "I am not the secretary if I can't get good material."

Maniac draped his arm over her shoulders. "Did you really think it was going to be what you thought it was?"

"Well, a girl can dream, can't she?" Wren reached over the bar and grabbed a glass. "Fill me up with Coke."

She slammed it down in front of Alice then plopped back down on the stool.

"No booze?" Alice asked,

Wren shook her head and glanced at Maniac. "Not for the next seven months."

Karmen jumped off her stool and pointed at Wren. "I freaking knew it!"

Karmen threw her arms around Wren and jumped up and down. Nikki hopped off her stool and joined in the jumping and celebrating.

I watched as Alice filled Wren's glass then set it down in front of the three of them that were going crazy. "Join the club."

Wren, Nikki, and Karmen froze mid-yell and looked at Alice. "Club?" they said in unison.

Alice looked at Wrecker who was now pale as shit and looked like he was ready to pass the hell out.

Holy fuck monkeys.

"What club?" he asked quietly.

Alice's eyes glassed over, and she sniffled. "Why do you think I bought these pants?"

"Uh, 'cause they're cow?" Pipe guessed.

Alice wiped her nose with the back of her hand. "Well, yeah, but also because they're fucking huge which means they'll have plenty of room for my stomach that is going to get as big as a basketball."

Wrecker sprang up from the table and catapulted himself over the bar. He wrapped his arms around Alice and pulled her into him. "You bought these pants two weeks ago," he growled.

"Yeah, well. I knew but didn't know how to tell you." Alice buried her face in Wrecker's neck. "I was also afraid it would come out with a beard like yours. It was a terrifying thought."

Wrecker roared with laughter and twirled Alice around in his arms. "You're having my baby," he yelled.

The card game was completely forgotten as everyone hugged and talked at once.

"You all right?"

I glanced over at Clash. "Never better." I drained my beer and set it down. "Why aren't you over there celebrating with them?"

He shrugged. "I'll tell them congratulations later. Probably when they're not going crazy."

I raised my eyebrow. "You do know you are talking about Alice, right?"

He chuckled and shook his head. "I know."

Crazy was the regular when she was around. "I think I'm gonna head to my room."

He looked at me then glanced at everyone else. "You don't want to hang around and congratulate your brother?"

I shook my head. "I'm like you. I'll wait 'til the crazy settles."

I watched Wrecker shake Pipe's hand with Alice still in his arms. He was happy. I didn't want to take that away from him. I wasn't something that made Wrecker happy.

Clash nodded. "I'll see you in the morning, beautiful."

My eyes dropped to the table. "Night, warden."

I slipped away from the table—no one noticed I left—and walked to my room.

I was foolish and looked behind my shoulder to see if anyone followed me.

No one was there.

I put my key into the lock and hesitated a second to listen for the mention of my name.

No one said it.

I closed my eyes and twisted the key.

No one knew I left because at the end of the day, no one cared.

*

Chapter Six

Clash

Ten minutes.

I stood outside her door for ten minutes trying to get the courage to knock.

I saw it in her eyes.

I saw the hurt.

I saw the pain.

Raven was hurt, and I saw it clear as day.

She had her radio on too loud, and some chick crooned through the door.

"What the hell are you doing?"

I looked down the hall and saw Brinks standing there in his underwear.

"What the hell are you doing?" I parroted.

Brinks reached down and itched his junk. "I was gonna grab a beer from the kitchen but instead, I've been standing here for five minutes watching you raise your hand only to lower it. You've done it seven times."

I moved away from Raven's door. "I don't know what the hell I'm doing."

"Looks like you want to talk to Raven but either your arm is broken, or you don't know what to say to her." Brinks looked around me. "I'm going to assume you don't know what to say to her since your arm seems to be okay right now."

"Alice and Wren are both pregnant." I didn't want to keep talking about me. Blurting out something completely off topic was exactly what needed to be done.

"That's what all the fucking shouting is about?"

I nodded. "Yeah. Alice surprised the hell out of everyone, even Wrecker."

Brinks chuckled. "Not surprising seeing the way Alice is."

I nodded and shoved my hands in my pockets. "Uh, I guess I'll get to bed."

It was only half past ten, but with Raven already in her room, there really wasn't anything for me to do.

Before I hadn't noticed it, but my life really did revolve around Raven.

Brinks looked at me knowingly. "Surprised you're not celebrating with everyone."

I shrugged. Everyone really was down there except me and Brinks. Well, Boink and Mayra were still gone 'til tomorrow, but even Freak and Slayer were drinking and acting like everything was amazing.

"I did for a bit."

Brinks looked at Raven's door. "But the person you really want to hang out with isn't down there."

My eyes connected with Brinks'. "No," I said loudly.

He shook his head. "Right, no." He smirked and turned back to his door. "Definitely not."

"Not, Brinks. Fucking not."

It wasn't that I didn't want to be with Raven, it was just weird to not have her down there.

That's what it was. It wasn't anything else.

"You've still got an hour or two to stare at her bedroom door. I'll let you get back to it."

"What about you?" I asked. "Why aren't you down there?"

He was acting like it was off that I wasn't down there, but his ass wasn't down there either. Though, he wasn't staring at someone's door instead of being with everyone else.

"The person I want to be with isn't down there either." He walked back into his room and shut the door. The lock clicked into place loudly, and the small crack of light from under his door went out. "Though I'm not staring at her door like a psychopath," he shouted through the door.

I hung my head and closed my eyes. "I'm not a psychopath," I mumbled.

"Right!" Brinks shouted.

I turned on my heel and stalked to my room without looking at Raven's door. She was locked in her room for the night, and I didn't need to worry about her.

The fact she didn't want to celebrate with everyone shouldn't be surprising to me. It wasn't like she hung out with them all of the time. Hell, I should have been concerned by the fact that she wanted to play poker with us tonight.

Normally, she was trying to find ways to not even come out of her room. Those were the times I was thankful to watch her because she wasn't getting into trouble.

I flipped on my light and flopped onto my bed.

This wasn't odd behavior from Raven.

Why the hell was I acting like it was?

She didn't want to be around her brother and the club.

That was fine.

What wasn't fine was the hurt in her eyes.

That wasn't fine at all.

*

Chapter Seven

Raven

"We should try to get something that is color-neutral," Mayra muttered.

"I'll have a salted caramel latte with a triple shot of espresso and two chocolate croissants. If you can make that latte the size of a bucket, I'll love you for the rest of my life."

The cashier smirked and grabbed my money. "I'll see what I can do, but I don't think bucket is a size."

I shrugged and turned back to Mayra who was still babbling about baby colors and shit.

"We could do a zoo theme." She tapped her finger to her chin. "That can definitely go both ways."

It had only been two weeks since Alice and Wren had dropped the bomb that they were both pregnant, but the clubhouse and all the ol' ladies were buzzing about the news. We had at least four months before we even needed to start planning the damn baby shower, but that was all anyone could talk about. Mayra included.

"Going both ways is always good."

Mayra kept talking, not even giving my lame joke a smile.

Clash stepped in front of me and ordered from the cashier.

I watched as her eyes flared with interest, and she leaned toward Clash as he placed his order. The woman would be putty in his hands if he let her know he was the teeniest bit interested.

Clash was in his usual attire of a white t-shirt and dark blue jeans that hugged his thighs and tapered off around his black motorcycle boots. Of course, he had his Fallen Lords cut draped over his shoulders, which for this chick, was the cherry on top of the sundae.

Surprisingly, Clash paid her no mind, just ordered his black coffee with an extra shot and handed her a five-dollar bill.

Mayra and I found a table toward the back of the coffeeshop, and Clash moved to sit at the one next to us.

"There something wrong with sitting with us?" I asked.

Clash's eyes connected with mine. "Didn't know if you were having a mini Girl Gang meeting or something."

I rolled my eyes and pulled out my chair. "I hope not. Sit with us so I have someone to talk to in case it is." Cora, Nikki, and Karmen were supposed to join us too, and as much as I didn't want to admit it, I knew this was a Girl Gang meeting. "You roped me into going out so you're going to have to suffer through this with me."

"Oh, there's Nikki and Karmen. I'll be right back." Mayra weaved through the maze of tables and gave a little screech when she hugged Nikki and Karmen.

"They do know they just saw each other last night, right?" I plopped down in my chair and dug into my croissants.

"Guess that's what chicks do," Clash mumbled. He had pulled out the chair next to me and had snapped off the lid to his coffee.

"Uh, pretty sure that's not what *all* chicks do." I rolled my eyes and ripped off a piece of flakey, gooey, chocolatey goodness.

"Well, all chicks but you."

"And thank God for that," I mumbled.

"Agreed, beautiful."

Clash had been calling me that since I had gotten my hair done.

I didn't know if I liked it. It was an endearment that was a bit too friendly. While I called him warden or biker boy, they didn't seem as personal as beautiful.

"You're glad I'm not some screeching woman?"

He chuckled and nodded. "Exactly."

I sipped my coffee and glanced at him out of the corner of my eye. "You've been rather agreeable lately."

"That a bad thing?" he drawled.

Was it? Clash and I hadn't butted heads since the day I had gotten my hair done. Granted, I had been so swamped with work the past week that I had barely had time to breath, let alone cook up ways to keep Clash on his toes.

"I guess it's okay."

"You've been the one who's been working her ass off. I'm waiting for the armored truck to pull up to the clubhouse with the pile of money you've been making."

"Slightly over exaggerated," I whispered. Though my bank account was sitting pretty plush right now.

"Right, beautiful. I've seen the shit you do on that computer. You're making bank," he said quietly.

Mayra and the girls made their way over to the table before I had to confirm that I was, in fact, rolling in dough.

"I saw the cutest onesie when I was at the store yesterday." Karmen dropped her wallet on the table and sprawled out in the chair across from me. "Nickel told me I wasn't allowed to buy it." She rolled her eyes and sipped on her coffee.

"Uh, that's probably because you already bought enough clothes for each baby to get them through until they are two." Nikki set her icy drink down and peeled off her coat. "You really need to slow your roll. At least until we find out what they are both having."

I could only imagine how crazy everyone was going to get when they found out if they were going to be boys or girls.

"I hope Alice has a boy and Wren has a girl." Mayra sipped on her coffee. "Only because I want a front-row seat for the next six months while Alice freaks out about the baby coming out with a beard."

I rolled my eyes and kept my mouth shut. Alice was going to worry about that even if she found out she was going to have a girl. This morning, she had been freaking out about possibly giving birth to the bearded lady or some shit.

The talk around the table revolved around the impending babies, and I could feel my eyes glaze over. Clash stayed quiet next to me, but I could tell he too wasn't keeping up with the baby talk.

I scooted my chair back, and Clash's hand was on my arm before I could even stand up.

"Where are you going?" he asked quietly.

"Bathroom, warden. That okay?"

He let go of my arm and sat back in his chair. "Yeah."

I rolled my eyes and made my way to the bathroom behind us.

Just when I thought Clash was chilling the hell out, he acted like he was personally in charge of making my decisions for me.

I did my business in the bathroom and was surprised as hell when I walked out that Clash was waiting for me in the little hallway.

"Really, warden? Did you think I was going to make a run for it or something?" I rolled my eyes and moved to walk past him, but his arm came out and blocked my path.

He caged me in with his arms and pressed me against the wall. "No. I wanted to make sure you were okay."

I laid my hands on his chest and tried to push him out of the way. "Never better. Out of the way, human wall."

The man was just a wall of muscle I wasn't able to budge.

"No."

I looked up into his eyes. "Excuse me?" What in the hell was this?

"We're gonna talk."

I blinked slowly. "Talk?"

"Yeah."

We stared at each other without speaking.

After thirty seconds of studying his handsome face and falling into the dark depths of his brown eyes, I blinked rapidly. "What the hell is going on, Clash?"

"I don't have a fucking clue."

"Then let me go."

He shook his head and somehow moved closer. His body was pressed against mine and his face was barely inches away from mine.

"Something is wrong."

Huh, yeah. Clash was way too close to me. His breath lingered with mine, and my mind was fogged. His musky, manly smell surrounded me, and it took all of my willpower to not bury my nose in the collar of his shirt and inhale.

"What's wrong?" My mouth felt like it was filled with cotton, and I could barely swallow.

"You're not happy."

I didn't deny it.

"Even when you were a bitch doing shit to annoy the hell out of me, I could tell it gave you a little bit of joy. Now, for the past two weeks, you're not happy. You don't take joy in annoying me or being a bitch to everyone. You're quiet and trying to fade away."

"That's ridiculous."

I was fine. Everything was fine. I was just swamped with work and didn't have the time to dedicate to being a bitch.

"It's not, Raven. Something changed when you found out Wrecker and Alice were pregnant."

I turned my head to the side. "No, nothing changed, Clash."

Everything was the same.

His hand cradled my cheek, and he turned my head back to look at him. "I saw it in your eyes, Raven. I saw something in them I've never seen before."

"And what was that?" I whispered harshly. I wasn't into this game Clash was trying to play with me. If he had something to say, then he needed to say it to me and not corner me in dark hallways.

"You're sad, beautiful. All this time, you wanted us to believe that you were just a bitch who doesn't give a fuck, but all along, you've just been sad and alone."

"No."

Clash's eyes slowly traveled over my face. "You are, beautiful. I see it. At first, I didn't. Thought you were just a bitch, but there is a hell of a lot more to you than what you show people."

I rolled my eyes. "Thanks, Dr. Clash. You ever thought of leaving the club and becoming a therapist?"

A smile spread across his lips. "You're the only one I have an interest in to care about."

"You shouldn't."

"I shouldn't what?" he asked.

"You shouldn't care about me."

"Why?"

I closed my eyes. "Because you would be the first."

"Raven," he whispered softly. His thumb gently stroked my cheek, and his arm wrapped around my waist. "Open your eyes for me, beautiful."

"No." I shook my head and tried to think of the weather or my coffee that was getting cold. I didn't want to think about this. I didn't want to feel Clash touching me.

I didn't want to open the vault of hurt that was buried deep inside me.

"I don't know what's happened to you, Raven. I don't know anything about you other than what you want me to know and see."

"There isn't anything else."

His warm lips pressed against my cheek. "There is more, Raven," he whispered in my ear. "There is a whole hell of a lot more, and I'm not going anywhere until I know it all."

"You're gonna be disappointed, Clash."

The things he wanted to know weren't fun. They weren't entertaining.

"I'll be the judge of that." His hand traveled down my waist and found my hand. He intertwined his fingers with mine and pressed another kiss to my cheek. "You lay it all on me, beautiful."

"And then you'll leave?"

That was what always happened.

Everyone always left.

"Guess you're just gonna have to wait and find out." He took a step back but his eyes stayed connected with mine.

"What in the hell are you doing, Clash?"

His fingers tightened around mine. "Staying."

He tugged me down the hallway, back toward the table.

"Let go of my hand," I hissed.

We literally had two seconds before we would clear the hallway and be in full view of Mayra and the girls. I didn't know what the hell was going on with Clash, so I really didn't want them to see us holding hands and want to know all of the details.

Clash let go of my hand at the last millisecond and strode back over to the table like he hadn't just rocked my world and turned it upside down.

"There you are," Mayra called. "I was starting to think you made your escape out of the bathroom window and Clash was chasing you down the street."

That would have been better than what had just happened.

"Not today. I couldn't get my butt through the small window." I nudged my chair away from Clash and sat back down.

"Caught her foot before she fell through."

Clash had seen me slyly move my chair and managed to also bump his closer to me when he sat down.

Mayra's jaw dropped. "Wait, what?"

I rolled my eyes. Bless Mayra's innocent soul. "I'm joking, Mayra."

"She's not." Clash winked at Mayra.

"Shut it, warden."

"There's that smile," he whispered so only I could hear him.

I was smiling. I hadn't even noticed. "Seriously, shut it," I hissed.

Clash chuckled but thankfully, didn't say more.

He had said more than enough back in the hallway. His words had been more than what I ever expected from him. Clash was seeing things that no one had ever seen before.

I wasn't sure how I felt about that.

Clash was seeing the me I had buried years ago, and I was absolutely terrified by what he was going to find.

*

Chapter Eight

Clash

"Are you seriously staring at her door again?"

"You just hang out by your door watching people?" I retorted.

Brinks leaned against the door frame and folded his arms over his chest. He was once again in his boxers looking like he had just woken up. "Trust me, I have better things to do. You obviously don't, seeing as you're staring at Raven's door like it's the gates of heaven."

I scowled. "If you've got something better to do, how about you go do it and leave me alone."

"Because then I can't give you my words of wisdom?"

I turned fully to look at him. "And just what are those?"

If he spit it out, he could leave me alone.

"Knock on the fucking door and stop fighting whatever shit that you got going on with Raven."

It had been four days since I had cornered her at the coffee shop, and Raven was the one who had been ignoring me. She was fighting whatever the hell this was, not me.

Though, I wasn't really sure what it was she was fighting.

"Thanks for the advice." I turned back to Raven's door. "Now, leave me the hell alone and go do whatever important shit you should be doing."

"Gladly," Brinks chuckled.

I heard his door close and raised my hand to knock on the door.

"Just fucking do it, Clash." I needed to just get this shit over.

For the past three nights, I had stood outside her door wondering what she was doing in there and wishing she would invite me in.

That was what was keeping me from knocking.

Would she invite me in or slam the door in my face?

There was only one way to find out.

I raised my hand and knocked.

*

Raven

Holy fuck was I bored.

Locking myself in my bedroom for the fourth day in a row was a good strategy to avoid Clash, but it was also boring.

So boring.

Of course, I came out to grab food, but as soon as I had what I wanted, I snuck back into my room and locked the door.

Clash had terrified me when he had cornered me at the coffee shop.

Not in the way that I thought he was going to hurt me, but in the way that he was going to see exactly who I was.

Who I had been hiding…

A knock sounded on the door, and my eyes darted toward it.

Who in the hell was knocking on my door?

Even Mayra didn't knock. She normally sent me a text asking what I was up to and telling me to unlock the door. I grabbed my phone, wondering if I had missed her text, but there was nothing.

"Who is it?" I called.

I waited a beat and then the voice I had been avoiding drifted through the door.

"It's Clash."

Shit.

"What do you want?"

Maybe the clubhouse was on fire and he was just telling me to get the hell out. I sniffed the air and was a tad bit disappointed to not smell smoke.

"For you to open the door."

"I don't have to."

I couldn't hear it, but I knew Clash had growled. Clash growling was something he did basically whenever I opened my mouth.

"Open the door, Raven, or I'll take it off the hinges."

"You wouldn't," I shouted.

"Fucking try me." His tone left no room for argument. Clash was going to come in if I opened the door or not.

I bounced off my bed, flicked open the lock, and swung open the door. "What?"

Clash planted a hand in my stomach, pushed me back, and slammed the door shut behind him.

"You're done hiding," he thundered.

"I'm not hiding. I'm working," I insisted.

"Why the hell can't you work in the common room like you used to?" he questioned.

"Because I don't want to."

Also, that was where Clash was. In my room, I was safe from him. Well, at least I used to be safe from him in here.

"Why?"

"Why what?" I shouted.

"Why in the hell don't you want to come out there?"

I crossed my arms over my chest and realized I wasn't wearing a bra. Hell, I was wearing barely any clothes at all. It was almost eleven, and I was dressed for bed.

"Get out so I can get dressed."

I was not going to be able to have this conversation with Clash when I was dressed in shorts that barely covered my butt cheeks and a thin tank top.

"You are dressed."

I rolled my eyes. "You would think that this was being decently dressed."

His eyes traveled up and down my body. "You look good."

"Clash," I growled through clenched teeth. "I am in my pajamas. Get. Out."

He shook his head. "Put a sweatshirt on or something, but I'm not going anywhere."

That would be doable if all of my sweatshirts weren't in the dirty laundry which was not in my room. This is what I got for waiting so long to do my laundry. I kept my arms over my chest and sat down on the edge of the bed.

"Say what you need to say and get out."

Clash sat down in my desk chair. "Pretty sure this isn't going to be that quick."

I rolled my eyes. "Then get on with it."

"Cut the attitude, Raven."

"Why? You don't get to come in my room and tell me what to do."

This was exactly what I had been wanting to avoid the past days.

"Because we both know it's fake. What I want to know is why you have to fake it."

A smirk spread across my lips. "You don't like when women fake it with you, Clash?"

Something in the air changed. I had gone too far. I wanted to grab my words and shove them back down my throat.

Clash shot up from his chair and pushed me back on the bed. He pinned me to the mattress with his body and caged me in with his arms.

"Never had a woman fake it with me before, Raven, and you sure as fuck aren't going to be the first." He was breathing hard, and his nostril flared as he stared down at me. "Cut the fucking shit."

"I don't want to." I didn't want to bare everything to Clash. No one had ever seen that before.

"Clue in, beautiful, you don't have a choice when it comes to this. You're not going to hate me and treat me like I'm a piece of shit when the way you feel hasn't got anything to do with me."

"And just who do you think it has to do with?" I hissed.

"Wrecker. Your family. Anything but me. You can't hate me, Raven, because I haven't done anything to you. All I want to do is keep you safe and happy."

"Pretty sure you only have to keep me safe, Clash. Wrecker could give a shit about the fact of whether or not I'm happy."

"There," he growled.

"There what?"

"Start there. Start there telling me why Wrecker doesn't care if you are happy or not."

"Because he didn't care when my parents died, so why in the hell would he care now?" I spat.

"Because he's your brother."

"Brother?" I laughed hysterically. "That's just a word, Clash. I can say a ton of words and they don't mean anything. I can call myself a fucking queen but that doesn't actually make me one. He had a chance to be the definition of the word brother, and he didn't. He chose this fucking club instead of being my brother. He choose *you* over me!"

The words poured out of me without even thinking about them. They were words that rolled around in my head constantly.

Wrecker may be my brother by blood, but when it came down to it, he was just a stranger.

"What happened?" Clash's eyes never left mine.

"It was either live with Wrecker or go into foster care. They were going to give me to Wrecker, and he told them no. He told them no!" Tears were flowing from my eyes, falling backward onto the bed. "He didn't want me!"

A knock sounded on the door. Both of our heads snapped toward it.

"Who is it?" Clash thundered.

"Open the fucking door."

Why in the hell was Wrecker knocking on my door? He was the last one I wanted to see right now. I'd much rather spend the rest of my life locked in here with Clash than see him.

"Go away," I screeched.

"You're in here fucking screaming," he yelled back. "Open the goddamn door."

"He's making sure I'm not hurting you, Raven," Clash said quietly.

I had been screaming, and it was somewhat late. "I'm fine, Wrecker. Leave me the hell alone."

The door handle rattled. "Open. The. Door."

Clash rolled off me and whipped open the door.

Wrecker pushed past him before I could even move off the bed.

"What in the fuck is going on in here?" Wrecker demanded.

I shook my head. "Nothing. I'm fine. Get out."

I wasn't going to go into this with Wrecker. There was no point in it. I had tried to talk to him about it years ago, but he didn't care. He didn't see things the way I did. He claimed to this day he had done the best thing for me.

He was so wrong, he didn't even know.

Wrecker looked at me splayed out on the bed and Clash who was standing by the door. "You lay one fucking hand on her and you'll never walk again."

"Like you fucking care," I spat. "If I want Clash, I'll fucking have Clash. You don't have a say in my life."

"I don't, do I? You might want to look around and realize who is keeping your ass safe right now." Wrecker jabbed his thumb into his chest. "I'm the one who fucking saved you."

"You saved me from the shitty ass situation you put me in when you asked me to go to work for The Ultra."

"I asked you to work for The Ultra, Raven, but your mouth was the thing that got you into trouble. That has nothing to fucking do with me."

I rolled my eyes and sat up. "Get. Out. I don't want you in here. You don't listen to a word I say."

"Oh, I hear you, Raven. The problem is, you only see your side of the story and don't care about mine."

I closed my eyes. "I've heard your side, Wrecker, but you don't want to hear mine."

"I've heard it! You think I left you. That I didn't want you! How was I supposed to take a fifteen-year-old when I didn't have a place to live? I didn't have two fucking nickels that were mine to rub together. I had nothing, but you don't see that. You only see the things that piss you off. The things that make you look right and me look wrong."

"That's all I see?" I jumped off the bed and got in Wrecker's face. "You wanna know exactly what I see?"

"I already know," Wrecker growled.

I clenched my teeth then let loose what had never been spoken. "His eyes were brown." My tone was even, but even as I spoke, I felt the panic come to the surface. "If I closed my eyes, he would hit me until I opened them. When I first moved in, he didn't come close to me. I thought he hated me because I was taking his mom and dad from him. He didn't touch me until I had been there forty-seven days. Forty-seven days," I enunciated slowly. "He didn't rape me until I unlocked my bedroom door and thought I was safe. When I close my eyes at night, I see his brown eyes. When I open my eyes, I see his brown eyes. I see his brown eyes!"

I shook with rage as tears rolled down my cheeks. My hands were clenched at my sides and my fingernails dug into the flesh of my palms. "While you were building your life and forming your brotherhood, your actual family was the plaything to a sick and demented psycho I couldn't escape."

The air crackled in the room, and the only thing I could hear was my heart beat thrumming in my ears. I had finally spoken the words that haunted me for the past ten years. "Get out of my room and get out of my life. There is no room for you and your *family* in it," I spat.

Wrecker didn't move. He stared me down as if he couldn't believe the words I had just said.

"GET OUT!" I screeched.

Clash moved from the door and got between Wrecker and me. "Leave, brother," he told Wrecker.

"Brother," I cackled. "You're not a fucking brother. You're an asshole who only cares about himself! A brother wouldn't send his sister away to be raped. Would you do that to Alice?"

Wrecker's chest heaved, and he leaned into me. "I didn't know! How was I supposed to know?!"

I sat back down and shook my head. "Didn't have a phone, did you? No way for you to get in touch with me?"

Clash caught Wrecker and pushed him toward the door. "You need to go right now."

"I'm not fucking leaving."

"You don't leave, she will, Wrecker. Decide what you really want."

"I didn't know," Wrecker said quietly. "If I would have known, I would have fought harder for you." Wrecker tried to take a step toward me, but Clash held him back.

"Just let her be right now. Just go." Clash pushed him toward the door, and this time, he moved. "Find Alice and go to bed."

Wrecker didn't take his eyes off me, and even though I wanted to look away, I stared at him until Clash shut the door in his face.

Clash turned to look at me with concern. "I don't know what to fucking say right now."

I flopped back onto the bed. "Neither do I, Clash."

I sighed and closed my eyes.

I had finally said it, and now I was going to have to deal with all of the other shit on the other side of hiding it.

Pity.

Sympathy.

Disgust.

All things I felt for myself on a daily basis.

"Can we go back in time? Change everything?"

"Much as I wish we could, beautiful, we can't."

I wiped my tear-stained cheeks with the heels of my palms. "How about for tonight? Can we just forget it until the morning?"

Clash sighed.

I leaned up and saw him standing at the foot of my bed. "You look extremely helpless right now, Clash."

"That would be because I am helpless, Raven. You just said what you said, and I don't have one fucking clue what I'm supposed to say to you right now." His arms were hanging at his sides with his hands clenched. "That's why you always had your door locked."

I laid my head back down. "Yes."

"That would never happen to you here, Raven."

A heavy sigh escaped my lips. "Sure, it wouldn't."

"I'm serious. Not one of these guys here would ever force themselves on you."

And I knew that. As much as I hated Wrecker for leaving me like he did, I knew that he would never surround himself with men like that.

"Wanna watch a movie?" Yes, I was fully trying to avoid this conversation.

Exploding like a volcano with Wrecker had completely exhausted me, and I didn't want to talk about it anymore with Clash.

"That really what you want, beautiful?"

"You really care what I want?"

"If I didn't care, I wouldn't be here right now."

I dug deep to try to find a bitchy reply but I had nothing. "Then put on a movie and stop talking."

That was all I had in me.

I listened to Clash move around my room. "Uh, where are the movies?"

A smile curved on my lips. "Grab the remote and point it at the TV. All of my movies are on demand."

"Fancy," he muttered.

"Were you looking for an actual movie?"

"Well," he drawled. "Yeah."

"Welcome to the future, Clash." I scooted up the bed and grabbed the remote from the nightstand. "Have at it."

I tossed the remote to him and laid down closer to the edge of the bed to leave room for him. I turned on my side with my arm under my head and watched as he sat back down on my desk chair.

"How the hell do you have all of these movies?"

I glanced at the TV. "I like to have the TV on while I work."

"And you work a lot so that explains why you would have so many damn movies."

I rolled my eyes and laid my head back down. "Are you going to sit over there?"

"Planned on it," he murmured.

I could sit in that chair for hours working, but even I knew my bed was much more comfortable. "You can lay on the bed, Clash."

"I'm good right here, beautiful." He had the remote pointed in the direction of the TV, and his brow was furrowed in concentration. "I can pick whatever?"

"Sure." All the movies he had as options were ones I had already watched so it wasn't like he was going to pick something I didn't like.

"You sure you're okay?"

I looked over him. "Perfect. Not like I just told a secret I'd been keeping for years or anything."

Clash chuckled and finally picked a movie. He tossed the remote on the bed next to me. "We can talk, if you want."

I shook my head. "I'll pass."

"Whatever you want." Clash leaned back in the chair and kicked his feet up on the desk.

"Thanks, Clash," I said softly. He could have been a real asshole with everything that just went on. Instead, Wrecker was the one being an asshole, and Clash was just trying to protect me. "You can go back to your room, if you want."

He shook his head. "I'm good here." He tucked his arms behind his head and kept his eyes on the TV. "Get some rest, Raven. I've got the door locked."

"Okay." I didn't need to have the door locked when he was in here with me, but it was nice that he thought I might need that. "But you really don't have to stay if you don't want to."

"You told me to sit down and shut up and now you're the one who won't stop talking."

I rolled my eyes. "I'm just letting you know I don't need you in here."

There was a little bit of that bitch dust I liked to spread around.

"Never said you did. But since you showed me all of these fucking movies you have just waiting on your TV for me to watch, it's gonna be a long while 'til you get rid of me."

Clash jumped up to turn off the light then settled back into his chair. He toed off his boots then kicked his feet back up on the desk.

This was different.

Normally, I worked until I was exhausted then fell into bed just to do it all over again the next day.

Now, I had Clash in my room watching a movie and Wrecker somewhere in the clubhouse more than likely telling everyone my business.

I closed my eyes and burrowed my head into my pillow.

That was too much for me to think about right now.

Tonight, I was just watching a movie with Clash and nothing had changed.

Tomorrow I would deal with the ensuing shit storm.

*

Chapter Nine

Clash

"Doesn't your neck hurt?"

I cracked open one eye. "Huh?"

"How in the hell are you sleeping like that?"

I opened both eyes and slowly moved my head. "Yeah, that fucking hurts."

Raven was standing over me with her nose crinkled up. "Well, that's not surprising. It looked like you were decapitated when I woke up this morning."

My head had been cranked all the way over the back of the chair, and I was going to pay dearly for it today. "Guess I can sleep anywhere."

Raven took a step back, and I stood. I rolled my neck back and forth, trying to work the kinks out of it.

"You could have slept in the bed with me."

I probably should have, but after the bombshell Raven had dropped last night, I didn't want to do anything that she wasn't completely okay with. "I'm good, beautiful."

"Right," she drawled.

"What time is it?" It felt like I hadn't even slept an hour.

"Six thirty."

"Say what?" Why in the hell were we awake this fucking early?

"I have plans today." I nodded to the chair he had been sleeping in. "Plans that involve that chair for a little bit."

Oh, hell. She needed to work and I was in her way.

I stepped to the side and reached for my boots. "Sorry, beautiful. I didn't know you got to work this early in the morning."

She laughed and shook her head. "Uh, I'm not going to work. I'm going to look for a place to rent."

"Say what?"

"You can lay in the bed if you want to hang around. I might need some help figuring out where to look since I don't want to wind up living by some psychopath or something."

I dropped my boots back on the floor. "You're moving?"

She sat down in the chair and swiveled around to face her desk. "Yeah. I woke up and decided that was what I needed to do."

"You can't."

She glanced over her shoulder at me. "Um, why not?"

"Because I'm supposed to keep you safe."

She rolled her eyes and turned back around. "There isn't anything that is coming to get me, Clash. I mouthed off to The Ultra, not killed Oakley Mykel's dog or something. I'm small fish to them."

She was right. I knew Wrecker was still concerned about The Ultra because he knew at the end of the day, they would do whatever the hell they wanted, but if they were that concerned with Raven, they would have already come after her.

"So, you're just going to leave."

"Well, yeah. I mean, I like Weston so I figured I would find a place here." She turned on her computer. "I just need help finding a place."

I watched her slowly spin around.

Gone was the woman who had angrily screamed at Wrecker.

In her place was a woman looking to run away and who didn't seem to have a care in the world.

"Don't you think maybe you should think about this for a second?"

She shook her head. "No. I don't need to think about it, Clash. I can't stay here for the rest of my life. Sharing a kitchen with nine grown men and their girlfriends isn't ideal. That's college."

"No, it's an MC."

She tipped her head to the side. "An MC I want no part of."

She saw the MC in a bad light, though. Not that she wasn't justified in seeing it that way, but I knew there was more to an MC than what she thought. I was going to have to convince her that while the decision Wrecker had made was the wrong one, she couldn't hold onto that forever. I saw Wrecker's face last night. He was gutted when Raven had blurted out the words. He didn't know one bad decision he had made had set Raven down the path to hell.

103

I sat down on the bed and laid back. "Tell me what you find, and I'll let you know if it's a good place to live."

"Really?"

I put my hands under my head and closed my eyes. "Sure."

It wasn't like Raven was going to find a place to move in to today. It was the middle of the month, and Weston was a smaller town. There weren't going to be many choices.

If Raven were to move now, I knew she wouldn't work through all the hurt she had about Wrecker. I need a little bit of time to help her move on and out of the clubhouse. It put a time crunch on that happening, but I liked a challenge.

Raven was definitely a challenge I was up to tackle.

*

Chapter Ten

Raven

"I feel like I need a shower."

Clash chuckled and threw his leg over the bike. "Same, beautiful."

I climbed on behind him and wrapped my arms around his waist. "I thought you were helping me find a nice place. That was infested by bugs and smelled like cat pee."

"You didn't really give me many options." He cranked up the bike and pulled away from the curb.

"One more place, right?" I yelled over the roar of the engine.

He nodded.

I watched the houses fly by and wished one of them could be mine.

I woke up this morning craving something I never had before. I wanted a place that was mine. Not a place shared by tons of people or just sleeping on random couches. I had the urge to put down roots.

"Stop!"

Clash pulled off to the side of the road, and I hopped off the bike. I jogged back two houses and stood in front of the place where I was going to put roots down.

"What the hell are you doing, beautiful?" Clash called.

I pushed my sunglasses on top of my head. "I want this," I shouted.

Clash slid off the bike and slowly made his way over to me.

"That's a house, beautiful."

"It is?" I gasped sarcastically. I turned back to look at the small two-story. "I want it."

Clash stood next to me and looked at the house. "It's blue."

I looked up at him. "Your eye for detail is astounding."

I pulled my phone out of my pocket and punched in the number to the realtor on the sign.

"What are you doing?" he asked.

I rolled my eyes and put the phone to my ear. "Ordering a pizza."

"Such a smart mouth," he chuckled.

The realtor answered the phone, and five minutes later, I had an appointment to view the house at two.

"You sure about this?" Clash asked.

I looked up at the house. It had a wraparound porch on the front and an attached two-car garage. "Well, I know I want to look at it." I slid my glasses over my eyes. "We view the house, and if it's a pile of poo, it's no skin off my teeth."

"All right, beautiful. You're calling the shots here."

This is what I was surprised with when it came to Clash.

He was laid back.

He listened to me.

He cared about what I said and felt.

He was the exact opposite of everything I thought he was.

"We grab lunch and then come back here for the viewing?"

He nodded and rubbed his stomach. "Works for me."

Without even thinking about it, I threaded my fingers through his, and we strolled back to the bike. I held on tightly as we made our way through town to the local diner and just enjoyed being with Clash.

A waitress seated us in a booth at the back of the diner, and I opened my menu.

"Buying a house seems like a pretty permanent move."

I didn't look up. "Yeah."

Clash grabbed my menu and tossed it down on the table. "Get the special. You won't be sorry."

"You're going to order for me?" Though I had planned on getting the special. Everyone knew at these little hole in the wall diners that was always your best bet.

Clash sat back in the booth and laid his arm along the top. "Can we talk?"

"About?"

"I got a fucking list of the shit we need to talk about, Raven. Where you wanna start?"

"Somewhere that isn't gonna make me too upset to eat my food."

Clash chuckled. "Can't guarantee that won't happen."

"Then I'm not interested in talking."

"Listen then."

I rolled my eyes and took the wrapper off my straw. "You're like a woman, obsessed with talking about everything."

"Because if you keep all of this shit bottled up, you're gonna become a raging bitch even I can't figure out how to handle."

I stuck my straw into my ice water. "But you have a new plan. One you tried on me the other night."

A plan, that at the time I didn't like, but with each minute I spent with Clash, I seemed to be more open to being with him.

"I don't think my good looks and charm would be enough to break through that bitch shield you're so good at throwing up."

"Bitch shield," I laughed. "Is that some kind of superpower? Do I get to wear a cape whenever I use it?"

"It should be a superpower with how good you are at it."

"Years of practice," I said with a wink.

"Wrecker texted me earlier."

I wiped the smile off my face. "Keep on with this, and I won't eat for a week."

"Wanted to know where we were and when we would be back."

He talked over my weak attempt to stop him. "Buying a house to get away from his controlling ass."

"You do know if you somehow manage to buy that house, it will be at least a month until you'll be able to move in, right?"

I shrugged. "At least I'll be able to have a countdown to my freedom."

"Back to Wrecker," he muttered. "I'm assuming he wants to know when we'll be back so he can talk to you."

I shook my head and signaled for the waitress to come over. "You think they serve beer here?"

"It's barely noon, Raven."

"Your point is?" I whispered. The waitress approached the table, and as much as I wished they served beer, they didn't. Clash and I both settled with Cokes and ordered the special.

"We didn't even ask what the special was."

Clash laughed and shook his head. "We'll find out soon enough."

His phone buzzed, and his brow furrowed as he read a text message. "I gotta be back for church at three."

"Oh yeah?"

Clash typed a reply on his phone then shoved his phone into his pocket. "Yeah."

"I get to know why you need to be back?"

He shook his head. "No."

"Well, I hope we're done looking at the house by then. Though, if you told me how important this meeting was, I could make sure we would be back in time."

Clash shook his head. "I don't know what the hell the meeting is about, beautiful. I'm in the dark as much as you are about it."

"Do you have any idea how annoying that is? My brother just sends a message and people just come running." I shook my head. "Absolutely pitiful."

"It's not pitiful. You just don't see the club from all sides."

The waitress brought our Cokes. "Food should be up in about five minutes."

I nodded, and Clash gave her a grunt. Neither of us were exactly overly friendly.

"And why should I have to see it from all sides, Clash? The side I'm on fucking sucks," I hissed.

He leaned forward and grabbed my hand. "I'm not saying your situation didn't suck. If I could go back and changed everything, I would, Raven. I would have been the one there for you."

I looked down at his hand. "That's sweet, Clash, but it really doesn't fix anything. My brother still choose the club over me. He didn't even fight for me because he was too busy building the club."

There wasn't anything that was going to be able to fix that.

"Raven," he said softly.

I looked up, and my eyes connected with his.

"I'm sorry that happened to you."

"Me too."

The waitress bustled over with our food and set down two plates filled with meatloaf, mashed potatoes, and green beans. "Two specials. Anything else I can get for you two?"

Clash let go of my hand, and I sat back in the booth. "A second stomach because there is no way I'm going to be able to eat this."

Clash chuckled. "I think we're good right now, but I'm sure she's going to want a to-go container."

I dug into my potatoes and let out a moan. "Sweet heavens, that is what carbs should taste like."

"Eat up, beautiful."

Clash and I managed to eat without talking about Wrecker or the club again. I just wasn't able to see things from his perspective. Wrecker was all about family and brotherhood when before he had formed the club, he didn't even fight to keep his blood family together.

How was I supposed to get past that?

*

Chapter Eleven

Clash

"You good with the girls?"

Raven looked up at me. "I'd rather just go to my room."

"Alice and Karmen seem pretty excited for you to hang out with them."

As soon as we had walked into the clubhouse Alice and Karmen had pounced on Raven to hang out with them.

She rolled her eyes and crossed her arms over her chest. "Probably because they want to grill me about what I said to Wrecker last night."

"I doubt they know, Raven."

A scoff escaped her lips. "You and I both know Wrecker told Alice and then she ran and told everyone else."

"I doubt that, beautiful. I don't think this is something Wrecker wants to broadcast."

She huffed and rolled her eyes again. "You're right. He wouldn't want to look like a hypocrite in front of his brothers."

I stepped closer to her. "Just try to be nice, and if it gets unbearable, just go to your room."

She tipped her head back to look at me. "I'm allowed to move without you following my every step?"

"Only if those steps take you to your room and nowhere else."

"This newfound trust in me is rather surprising."

I leaned closer. "It's not that I don't trust you, it's I don't know exactly what you're capable of."

"Like burning down the clubhouse?"

A smirk spread across my lips. "Now you were the one who brought it up this time, but yes, exactly."

Raven bumped her shoulder against mine. "Go meet with your boys. I promise to play nice until you get back."

"Not too nice. Then they'll know something is up."

"Right, right." She shook her head and headed over to the couch where some of the girls were sitting.

Brinks walked out of the kitchen with a sandwich in his hand. "You gonna come to the meeting or just stare at Raven all day?"

"I'm not staring at Raven."

"Really? Cause that is exactly what you are doing right now."

Raven plopped down on the couch next to Alice and flipped me off. "Get to church, warden."

"Even she busted you staring at her."

I turned on my heel and headed down the hallway. "Wasn't staring at her."

"Mmhmm," Brinks hummed. "Of course, you weren't."

We walked into church, and I took my usual seat between Brinks and Boink.

Wrecker walked into the room with Pipe and Nickel following behind.

Boink leaned toward me. "Wonder what this is going to be about. I thought shit was finally running smooth with The Ultra."

I had thought the same thing. Even shit with Leo Banachi had been laid to bed. There shouldn't be anything going on that required an out of the blue meeting.

"Shut the hell up, fucker." Pipe slapped Boink across the head and sat down next to him.

"Brother," Boink grumbled. He rubbed his head and flipped Pipe off. "You really had to hit me that hard?"

"Probably not," Pipe laughed.

"All of you shut the hell up." Wrecker grabbed the gavel next to his hand and slammed it on the table.

Slayer sat up straight and pointed to the gavel. "Uh, you actually used that."

"Shit must be going down," Brinks mumbled.

Wrecker dropped it on the table with a thud. "Actually, for the most part, shit is good. I just wanted to keep you idiots on your toes."

"Wait, what?" Poor Freak was still pretty new to coming church. He had only been a full member for a couple of months, and those couple of months had been crazy.

"Guns are up and running on the south side of town. Oakley and The Ultra seem to be assimilating into the town rather smoothly." Wrecker sat back in his chair. "As of right now, there isn't much they need from us. Once they start expanding further south, they'll be needing us for transportation."

"How long until that happens?" Nickel asked.

"Two or three months. Oakley has a large enough operation that I really don't think he'll be needing us that much." Wrecker cleared his throat. "Though there is something we need to remember."

"And here comes the news that some chick has been kidnapped and we need to go rescue her." Slayer laughed. "Which one of us is going to be sent to rescue the hot chick that's going to become our ol' lady?"

"Funny," Pipe chuckled.

Brinks shook his head. "I think that's the first funny thing you've actually said, Slayer."

"No one needs rescuing right now." Wrecker looked around the table. "Dealing with Oakley and the Banachi's pushed Jenkins to the back burner."

Pipe whistled. "That bottom feeder? What the hell is he doing?"

"Right now nothing, but there are rumblings."

"What kind of rumblings?" I asked.

Wrecker tapped his fingers on the table. "He's pissed about being pushed out of working with The Ultra."

"And he thinks he's going to do something about it?" Nickel shook his head. "That asshole dug his own fucking grave."

"I agree, but I think it's something that we need to keep an eye on. I want two of you to go to River Valley." Wrecker looked around the table again. "Don't all volunteer at once."

"What exactly do you want us to do? It's not like we can get close to Jenkins without him knowing we're with the Lords," Boink scoffed.

A rare smile crossed Wrecker's lips. "That's the thing. I want him to know you're with the Lords."

"Uh, why?" Nickel asked.

"This seems like a bad idea to me." Pipe held up his hands. Wrecker turned his head to glare at him. "But I am only the Vice Prez so perhaps I don't know it all."

"I'm trying to be proactive here. I want two of you to roll into River Valley and act like you are king fucking shit."

We all moved restlessly. This did not sound like something that would end well. Jenkins was a fucking psychopath who was always looking for the next big thing to line his pockets.

I leaned against the table. "Does Jenkins even have a club anymore?"

Last I heard, all of the members of the River Valley chapter of the Fallen Lords left because Jenkins was running the club into the ground.

"He's got a few guys that stuck around. The thing about Jenkins is, he's a fucking moron who thinks he's the best. While most of the time guys like him fade away, Jenkins seems to be staying afloat," Wrecker said flatly.

Slate shook his head. "This seems like we're trying to start some shit. Why not just leave the fuckwad alone and let him run himself into an early grave?"

"Because when fuckwads are left alone, they find other fuckwads to come make our lives a living hell." Wrecker sat forward. "Only Pipe and Nickel know Jenkins like I do so I understand why you guys aren't getting this. Jenkins was on the top of the world before I butted in and managed to make a deal with The Ultra that ultimately screwed Jenkins. Jenkins wants revenge, and I want to know it's coming before it actually does. Two of you are going. Thirty seconds to fucking decide or I decide who."

"Not it," Pipe hollered.

"I got a newborn. I'm not fucking going," Nickel said at the same time.

Boink held up his hands. "Wren is pregnant. No way in hell she is going to be okay with me basically moving to River Valley. Not it."

"I'm already keeping an eye on Raven." No way in hell I was going.

"Clash isn't going," Wrecker agreed.

"For fuck's sake," Brinks grumbled. "I'll fucking go. Freak or Slayer can alternate staying with me. We're the only three that don't have chicks waiting at home for us."

"So that's how it is?" Slayer laughed. "Gotta find me an ol' lady and then I don't have to go on these whack jobs?"

Pipe shrugged. "It wouldn't hurt for you to find a

woman, but there is the problem of your face that might make that kind of hard."

We all roared with laughter, and Slayer flipped off Pipe.

"Fuck you," Slayer grumbled.

Wrecker slapped the gavel on the table again. "That's decided. Brinks and Slayer are going to handle Jenkins. You guys can leave in the morning."

"Hey," Slayer protested. "I thought Freak was going to be a part of this clusterfuck?"

Wrecker shook his head. "Nah. Freak can hangout around the clubhouse to keep an eye on everything."

Slayer glared at Freak. "Must be nice to be the new guy in the club and get the easy fucking jobs."

"Pretty sure acting like your top shit for a couple of weeks is going to be a real hard job," Nickel laughed.

"Yeah," Pipe agreed. "Just act like you do here. That is, until Wrecker reels you in."

"As long as I don't have to take care of some chick while I'm there, it'll be all good." Slayer put his arms behind his head and sat back in his chair. "I guess I can see the silver lining in all of this."

"All right. That's it."

Everyone got up and slowly milled around.

"Clash," Wrecker called.

I knew this was going to happen. Though I had sort of expected it during the meeting. I tipped my chin to him and moved into the chair Pipe had been sitting in.

"Get the hell out, fuckers," Wrecker ordered.

The guys cleared out quickly, and Nickel pulled the door shut behind him.

"Where were you today?"

I rested my elbows on the table. "Out with Raven."

I wasn't really upset with Wrecker. He had done a shit thing to Raven, but I also knew there wasn't a way in hell he could have known what would happen to her.

"That's new," he rumbled.

"There were a couple of places she wanted to look at."

I didn't know if I should be telling Raven's business but I didn't really think it would matter to Wrecker.

"Come again?"

Or maybe he would care.

"She found a few apartments online to look at. They all turned out to be shit."

I was going to leave out the fact that the house we had looked at was exactly what Raven wanted, and I even had to admit that it was nice.

"She doesn't need to find a place to live."

"She really need to be in the clubhouse?"

She didn't want to be here, and there wasn't any threat against her. At least, not one I knew about.

"No, but she has the clubhouse. What's the sense in finding someplace else to live when she can live here?"

"Guess the same reason Alice, Karmen, Nikki, Wren, and Mayra have some place to live besides here."

"They aren't like Raven."

I sat back in my chair. "We both know what this is about, Wrecker."

"And just what do you think this is about?" he asked.

"You fucked up before, brother. Keeping her captive at the clubhouse isn't going to fix any of that."

"I didn't fuck up," he insisted. "I did what I thought was best for her."

I knew this.

I knew the type of man Wrecker was. If he had an inclination that Raven would have been hurt, he never would have let her go into foster care.

But he hadn't known. No one could have guessed that was going to happen to her.

"You think maybe you should be talking to her about this?"

I had finally started to break down the walls Raven had put up, and I didn't want to fuck it up by betraying her trust and telling Wrecker everything she had told me.

"Because last night went so well."

"Try not barging into her room."

"You were in her room," he replied. "Why the hell couldn't I be in there?"

I shrugged. "She wanted me in there. You, not so much."

"So you think you know my sister?" he growled.

I shook my head. "Not by a fucking longshot."

"Yeah, because I remember not too long ago, you were bitching to anyone who would listen that she was a bitch and would be the death of you."

There was no point in denying it. I had said all of those things and more, but that was before, when all I knew about Raven was the tiny bit she showed people. "Said it all, brother. Doesn't mean I can't change my opinion of her."

"Yeah, seemed like you definitely changed when I walked in on you two."

I folded my arms over my chest. "You mean when you barged in?"

"She had barely any clothes on, Clash. You really think it's a good idea to get tangled up with my sister?"

"Pretty sure you were the one who wanted me to keep an eye on her."

"An eye on her, Clash. Not your fucking hands."

I chuckled and shook my head. "You're walking a fine fucking line right now, brother. You might want to take a step back and think for a second."

Wrecker was my Prez when it came to the club, but he did not get say in everything in my life.

"She is my sister."

"You sure about that?" I couldn't help it. I couldn't keep the words in my mouth. "She needed you ten years ago, and you let her go without a fight. Sister or nuisance?"

Wrecker planted his hands on the table and pushed his chair back. It skidded on the floor and banged against the wall. "That how you see all of this?" he roared.

I quickly stood up and clenched my fists at my side. "I see this from both of your sides, Wrecker. The problem is, you're both stubborn assholes who can only see the side they are standing on."

I hadn't been lying to Raven when I told her that I got it from all angles.

"I had no choice," he rumbled. "What was I supposed to do? I didn't know they were going to stick her in some home with a fucking lunatic. I didn't know," he shouted.

"No one could have known but stop acting like you had no choice. You had choices. They might not have been amazing, but you had them. You could have forgotten the club and found a regular nine-to-five job and a place to live."

"That's not the life for me."

I knew what he meant. I felt it too. Nine-to-five was not the life meant for me either. I craved the unity and brotherhood of the club.

"I get that. But don't sit there and act like you had no choice. You had choices and went with the one that you thought was for the best. I would have made the same choice. The choice you made that I don't agree with is not checking on Raven. Making sure she was okay. You left her and didn't look back. One phone call or visit to that house might have saved her, Wrecker. You left her for years without any word to her."

Wrecker's chest heaved, and he breathed heavily. "I. Didn't. Know."

I shook my head. "And now you do know. What are you going to do about it?"

I walked out of church and straight to Raven.

She was sitting on the couch laughing at something Alice had said. Her eyes connected with mine, and she smiled wide.

Wrecker may not have chosen her back then, but I was going to be damned if I didn't choose her right now.

*

Chapter Twelve

Raven

"They accepted."

I cracked open one eye. "Huh?"

"My offer."

I closed my eye and tried to process what the hell Raven was talking about. "What time is it?"

"Four."

"In the morning?"

Her light laugh floated around me. "No. In the afternoon. You crashed while I was working."

That was a relief. I had been thinking I had slept all of the day away.

It had been a week since Raven had looked at her dream house and I had my disagreement with Wrecker.

In that time, she had managed to get preapproved for a loan and put an offer in on the house. Now, it sounded like it was hers.

"Okay, start from the beginning."

Raven flopped on the bed next to me and rested her head on her hand. "They accepted my offer," she repeated. "Closing will be in a couple of weeks, and then I can move in! I'm going to be free!" she shouted.

I put my hand over her mouth. "Whoa there, beautiful. I think maybe you should break the news to Wrecker in a better way than shouting it for the whole clubhouse to hear."

She rolled her eyes and knocked my hand away. "I couldn't care less what he thinks."

I knew she didn't care what Wrecker thought, but at the end of the day, he was still her brother.

"I'm happy for you, beautiful."

"You say that now until you have to help me move in," she giggled.

My fingers brushed against her bare arm. "Is that your subtle way of asking me to help?"

Things had stayed the same between Raven and me.

She was more open with me, and there was a slight sexual tension in the air. I wanted her. There wasn't any doubt about that, but I didn't want to push her. I didn't want her to think that I only wanted her because she was within arm's reach.

She laid her head down and smiled. "Perhaps?"

"Well," I mumbled. "I guess I need to know what I get in return."

She batted her eyelashes. "The warm fuzzy feeling in the pit of your stomach knowing you helped me without wanting anything in return?"

I chuckled and shook my head. "I think I might need a little bit more than that."

"Just a little bit more?" she whispered.

I scooted closer and draped my arm across her waist. "I'm pretty sure we can work something out that would make both of us happy."

She bit her lip, and she focused on my mouth. "Maybe…a kiss?" she whispered.

"You'd be happy with that?" I asked.

She nodded. "I wouldn't be upset about it or anything."

"You let me kiss you now, that means I'll probably kiss you later." I cleared my throat. "Fair warning."

"I like that warning."

"So do I." I threaded my fingers through her hair and pulled her close 'til my lips pressed to hers.

She melted into my touch and gasped lightly.

"Tell me to stop, Raven."

She shook her head. "Never." She rolled into me and pushed her body fully against mine. "Kiss me, Clash."

Those were the three words I had been wanting to hear the past two weeks. Those were words I couldn't say no to.

Her lips were like velvet beneath mine, and her soft whimpers drove me insane. Her hands traveled over my chest, and I pulled her on top of me.

"It sure is a nice view from up here," she whispered against my lips.

"It's not too bad for me either."

"Such a sweet talker," she giggled.

Her lips melded against mine, and I pulled the hem of her shirt up. Her warm skin was soft and silky beneath my fingers. "You feel like heaven."

She moaned and opened her mouth. My tongue slid inside, and her delicious taste went straight to my head.

"Why did we dance around this for two weeks?" she asked breathlessly.

"I think we both thought it was a bad idea, but right now, I don't know why we thought that."

A knock sounded on her door, and we both froze.

"No," she groaned.

"Just ignore it."

The fucking pope could have been knocking on the door and I wouldn't have answered it.

Whoever it was knocked again.

"Go away!" Raven shouted over her shoulder.

"Open the door, Raven."

"Was that Alice?"

That was not who I expected to be knocking on the door.

Raven dropped her forehead against mine. "Ugh. Yes."

"What the hell is she knocking on the door for?"

Raven sighed and lifted her head. "I told her I would go with her to her doctor's appointment. Wrecker had something going on, and he can't be there."

"Seriously?"

That surprised the hell out of me that Raven had agreed to go with her. Ever since Raven had opened up to me about her past, she had also opened up a bit with the other girls. Wrecker was a completely different story, though.

I could count on one hand the amount of words Raven had spoken to him.

"Is it hard to believe that she asked me?"

I laughed and shook my head. "Hard to believe that you said yes."

"Raven! We need to leave in two minutes. Put your pants on and let's go."

Raven's eyes bugged out.

"She's got her pants on," I shouted back.

"Then get your paws off of her and let me have my friend for two hours," Alice replied crankily.

"Does she have x-ray vision?" Raven whispered.

I rolled out from under her and stood up. "No, beautiful."

Though I did have to wonder how she knew I was even touching Raven.

"You two have been making googly eyes at each other for the last two weeks. Wrap it up and I promise you can continue it just as soon as we get back from checking on baby man."

"Is she really still calling her baby that?"

Raven chuckled and scrubbed her hands down her face. "Sure is. Though she does switch up the nickname now and then." She rolled off the bed and shoved her feet into a black pair of Converse. "I'm coming," she called.

"You need me to drive you to the doctor?"

Raven shook her head. "No. Cora is coming with us too so I think I'll be protected."

"The fact that Cora will keep you just as safe as I could is a little alarming."

She laughed and grabbed a black sweatshirt that was draped over her desk chair. "Please, you know between Cora and me, no one stands a chance."

I squinted. "Yeah, I would have to say, whoever messed with you two would have to be pretty dumb."

She grabbed her wallet and tucked it under her arm. "Does this mean I get a goodbye kiss now?"

I shrugged. "Only if you come and give me one."

She rolled her eyes but moved over to me. "You're kind of demanding." She reached up on her tiptoes and pressed her lips against mine. "But I like it," she whispered.

I swept her into my arms and kissed her like she was my next breath.

"Whoa," she gasped, breathless. "Save some of that for later, warden." She patted my on my chest and licked her lips. "Definitely later," she mumbled.

Raven walked out of the bedroom and winked at me over her shoulder.

"Later, beautiful."

Alice clutched a hand to her heart and sighed. "I know that look all too well."

Oh, hell. Maybe giving Raven a goodbye kiss wasn't the best idea. Now it was going to be all over the clubhouse by dinner time that Alice had interrupted us.

"Call me if you need anything," I called.

Raven nodded and threw another wink my way. "Will do, warden."

"You calling him warden now is a whole new level of kink I didn't even think of," Alice gushed.

Raven rolled her eyes and pulled the door shut behind her while Alice kept talking.

Now I had a good two or three hours without Raven around.

I looked around her room and laughed. "So this is what it was like before she came into my life."

Three hours of free time and all I thought about was what it would sound like if Raven called me warden during sex.

I figured out it would be hot as fuck.

*

Chapter Thirteen

Raven

"Any other questions?" The doctor looked between the three of us.

Alice had just gone through four pages of questions she had jotted down the past two weeks. If she had any more questions, they were going to be along the lines of what would happen if the baby came out as an alien, because she had asked every other possible question under the sun.

Alice shook her head, and the doctor took off out the door without a backward glance. She knew if she gave Alice time, she would be stuck in here for another fifteen minutes.

Cora grabbed the notebook out of Alice's hand and tossed it in the garbage. "You are damn insane."

"What?" Alice gasped. "I just asked the doctor all of the questions I had. Isn't that what she is here for?"

Cora bent forward and looked at me. "What happens if I take a bath? Do I have to stop eating peanut butter? And this one was my favorite. Are beards hereditary?"

I couldn't hold it back anymore. I blew out a raspberry and burst out laughing.

"I don't know why I thought coming to the doctor with you would be a normal experience. Being your friend sure the hell isn't, so why would this, right?" Cora grabbed her purse off the floor and tucked it under her arm. "I need a drink and possibly a cigarette."

Alice plugged her fingers in her ears. "You cannot talk about drinking. I've wanted a drink since I peed on that damn stick."

"You do know you can have a glass a wine or some shit like that, right?"

Cora and Alice both turned to look at me.

"How the hell do you know that?" Alice demanded.

I rolled my eyes and stood up. "I'm really surprised you didn't ask the doctor that."

"Because I didn't want them to take my baby away before I even had it," Alice muttered. "Now spill the beans on how you know I can have a glass of wine. I need proof to back up me doing this."

I held out my hand and pulled Alice out of her chair. She barely had a bump, but she was fully embracing the pregnant life.

"I heard it on one of those morning shows, and it was a big deal a couple of years ago. I'll Google it on the way home or I can call the doctor back in."

Alice rubbed her stomach and shook her head. "No. I need a foot-long sub and one of those big-ass fountain drinks."

"It has been ten minutes since you've eaten," Cora muttered. "Wouldn't want you to get hungry or anything."

In the middle of Alice asking the doctor every question under the sun, she had pulled out a bag of dried cranberries and a sleeve of crackers.

The woman had a snack while she rapid-fired questions at the poor doctor. I would be surprised as hell of the doctor didn't cancel her next appointment and suggest she find a new OB/GYN.

"We can stop on the way back to the clubhouse."

We made our way through the clinic and out to Cora's car. Alice sat in the front next to Cora, and I chilled out in the back.

I pulled out my phone and saw that Clash had texted me.

How's it going? It was from forty-five minutes ago.

I'm trying to figure out what I did before you came to the clubhouse. Thirty-nine minutes ago.

I think I was bored a lot. Thirty-seven minutes ago.

Or I was drunk a lot. Twenty-nine minutes ago.

Took the bike to fill it up. Nineteen minutes ago.

Just realized I'm texting you a fuck ton. Thirteen minutes ago.

Is it possible to erase messages before someone reads them? Ten minutes ago.

Fuck. I meant to ask Google that. Four minutes ago.

"Girl, what is with that huge ass smile on her face?"

I glanced up and saw Cora and Alice were both turned in their seats looking at me.

"She's been bit by the biker bug." Cora wiggled her eyebrows.

I curled my lip and dropped my phone in my purse. I most certainly had not been. "Uh, no."

Alice wiggled her finger at me. "I do not blame you. Clash's shoulders are amazing, and that smoldering look he has is enough to knock down anyone's walls."

"My walls are not knocked down," I insisted.

"They all say that," Cora laughed. "Though in the end, they always end up pregnant and happy." She hitched her thumb toward Alice. "Exhibit A."

Alice knocked her thumb down. "I didn't plan on falling for the bearded biker."

"You guys never plan it, but it always happens." Cora started the car and headed back to the clubhouse. "And then you always act surprised that it happened."

"Nothing is happening," I insisted.

Alice gave me a knowing look. "Right," she drawled. "There was nothing happening when I knocked on your door earlier." She wiggled her eyebrows. "Warden," she whispered.

I put my hand in her face and shook my head. "I'm going to need you to turn around."

"Why?" Alice laughed. "Am I hitting a little too close to home?"

I rolled my eyes. "I'm not going to be the next ol' lady to be instilled in the clubhouse. I'm getting my own place and getting the hell out of there."

"What?" Alice gasped. "How the heck did you convince Wrecker of that?"

I leaned forward. "I didn't ask, Alice. He may be my brother, but he has no say in what I do with my life."

"That's not what I meant." She wrinkled up her nose. "Well, that's sort of what I meant. I thought you were at the clubhouse because Wrecker is afraid something is going to happen to you."

I snorted. It was a little too late for that. "I'm there because my brother feels guilty."

"Guilty?" Cora glanced at me in the rearview mirror.

"What do you mean?" Alice asked.

I shook my head and looked out the window. "You're going to have to ask him that, Alice."

"You do know she is going to ask him, right?" Cora laughed.

I was actually surprised she didn't already know. "Ask him, Alice. Then come ask me again because I really doubt he's going to tell you the whole truth."

Alice looked concerned but didn't say anything else. She turned back around and cranked up the radio. "Don't forget to stop for a sub," she muttered to Cora.

I had killed the fun mood. I didn't mean to.

I guess since it was out there what had happened to me, I didn't feel like I needed to hide it anymore. Not that I was going to shout it from the rooftops, but I wasn't going to hide from it anymore.

Regret hit me almost instantly, though.

Was I really ready for the whole world to know what happened to me?

I had come to terms with it a while ago.

I stared out the window and sighed.

No going back now.

*

Chapter Fourteen

Clash

"She's not going to be able to eat all of that."

"You're wrong. I watched her eat a whole can of Pringles yesterday and then tell Wrecker ten minutes later she was dying from hunger." Nikki wiped her mouth with the back of her hand. "She's going to finish that sub and then grab the gallon of vanilla ice cream. Just watch," she muttered.

"Wrecker is going to have to go in the grocery business if he wants to keep up with Alice," Pipe chuckled.

Nikki elbowed him in the gut.

"What the hell was that for?" he rubbed his stomach and glared at Nikki.

"That wasn't nice," she grumbled.

"You're the one who just told us she ate a whole can of Pringles without coming up for air. I was just making an observation," Pipe grumbled.

I finished my beer and set it next to my three other empties. "Pretty sure making any kind of observation about what a woman is eating is not the right thing to do."

Nikki wagged her finger at me. "Clash is smart." She looked at Pipe. "Be more like Clash."

Cora chuckled. "Words I never thought I would hear."

"But she ain't wrong," I laughed.

Pipe flipped me off. "Shouldn't you be keeping track of your inmate, warden?"

Now it was my turn to flip him off.

"Call me warden again and you'll find my fist in your face."

Raven was the only one who could call me that. It had taken on a whole new meaning since she first used it.

"He's got amazing shoulders," Alice called. "I would listen."

"Woman," Wrecker growled.

"What?" Alice protested. "Have you not seen them? They're huge."

"Not sure I like you taking notice," Wrecker growled.

Alice rolled her eyes. "Your beard is better." She pointed at her stomach. "And, you're the one who got me pregnant. Pretty sure you've got nothing to worry about."

Wrecker looked at her stomach, and the hard lines around his eyes softened. "Just make sure it stays that way."

I grabbed my empty bottles and stood up. "I'm gonna check on Raven."

This was not a conversation I needed to stick around for. I dropped the empties into the garbage can and made my way to Raven's room while Alice kept talking about my shoulders.

Having the Prez's ol' lady talking about me was a little odd but when you factored in that it was Alice, it wasn't so odd.

I knocked on Raven's door and waited to hear the lock slide.

The first words out of her mouth made me chuckle. "Did she eat the whole thing?"

"Should have stuck around and found out for yourself." I stepped around Raven and fell back on her bed.

"I've slacked the past couple of days. I needed to get some work done." Raven shut the door and locked it.

I hated that she automatically locked it. Even though I had managed to scale the walls she had put up, she still didn't feel completely safe.

"She had less than half of it left." I put my arms behind my head and glanced at the TV. "You're watching this again?"

Raven snatched the remote off the bed and pointed it at the TV. "I can never get tired of *Aquaman*. If you have a problem with that, you can take your negativity somewhere else."

I chuckled and shook my head. "I think I'm good right here. Just wake me up when it's over."

Raven *hmphed*.

"You finish up what you needed to?" I asked.

She shook her head and sat down on the edge of the bed. "Hardly. I can't seem to concentrate. All I keep thinking about is the house."

"Wanna know what I keep thinking about?" I asked softly.

She glanced over her shoulder at me. "You gonna tell me or show me?"

I jackknifed up to sit and pulled her against my chest. "That an invitation?" I whispered.

She bit her lip and nodded. "Yeah. Because I think I might have thought about this exact thing a time or two since I got back."

"Thank God," I growled. I closed the gap between us and delved my fingers into her hair.

She straddled my lap and draped her arms over my shoulders. "Kiss me, Clash."

The kiss was rough and deep. Her lush body was pressed firmly against mine, and she ground her sweet pussy into my hardening cock. Her fingers found the hem of my shirt and pulled it over my head.

"Jesus," she gasped. Her hands were all over me, trying to feel everything at once. She pressed greedy kisses across my chest, and her tongue licked the curve of my collarbone.

"Holy fuck, Raven," I growled.

She hummed softly and planted her hand on my chest. "Holy fuck is right," she whispered. She pushed me back and fell, coming with me.

We were a flurry of hands trying to touch and feel. I was pulling her shirt up, and her fingers were on the zipper of my pants when a knock sounded on the door.

"No," she whined.

I squeezed my eyes shut and willed whoever had knocked to go the fuck away.

"Raven," Wrecker called.

"You gotta be fucking kidding me," Raven whispered.

"Your brother is a fucking cock-blocker," I grumbled.

She laid a finger on my lips. "Shh. Maybe he'll think we're sleeping."

I opened my mouth and sucked her finger in. She closed her eyes and moaned.

"Raven. We gotta talk," he called through the door.

Raven's eyes opened, and she shook her head. "Not happening," she whispered.

Raven and Wrecker needed to clear the air about everything that had happened in the past, but it didn't seem like Raven wanted to do that right now.

He knocked one more time, and Raven shook her head. "Should I answer it?" she asked.

I let go of her finger and growled. "Tomorrow."

She laughed and pressed a kiss to my chest. "I like the way you think."

My hands went back to her shirt, and I pulled it over her head before we could get interrupted again.

She popped open the button on my jeans and pulled the zipper down. "This is happening."

"Are you talking to me or my dick?"

"Both." Her eyes connected with mine and then she slide down my body. She tugged my jeans down and off my legs. She hooked her thumbs in the waistband of my boxers and pulled them down. My cock laid heavy against my leg, and my breath caught when her fingers wrapped around the shaft.

Her mouth was on me before I could even think, and she swallowed me deep. The warmth of her mouth surrounded me, and her eyes connected with mine as she bobbed up and down.

"Fucking shit, Raven."

She moved slowly, her tongue caressed every inch of my dick, and her hand cradled my balls. She rolled them between her fingers and moaned.

"So fucking beautiful." Watching my dick disappear in and out of her mouth was almost too much to take.

My cock slid from her mouth, and she stroked it with her hand.

"You like that?" she asked.

"You got no fucking clue, beautiful."

A smirk spread across her lips, and she watched a pearl of precum form on the tip of my dick. She leaned down and lapped it up with her tongue. She hummed and sucked the tip of my dick between her lips.

I was close to coming, and I hadn't even sunk my cock into her yet. She was going to have to catch up to me.

I grabbed her under her arms and hauled her up my body. "You trying to make me lose it?"

She licked her lips. "Maybe?"

"Payback's a bitch, beautiful."

I flipped her onto her back and had her pants and panties off before she could even breath. "Whoa," she gasped.

I slid down her body, pressing kisses to her soft skin along the way. "Wonder if you taste like this all over."

"Only one way to find out," she mumbled.

I glanced up and saw her eyes on me, her bottom lip between her teeth, and her arms behind her head. "Watch, beautiful. Watch me eat you."

I parted the lips of her pussy, and her body shook with anticipation.

My tongue teased her sweet clit, and my fingers plunged into her.

"Clash," she moaned loudly.

My name coming from her lips while I tasted her sweet pussy went to my head. This was something I wanted every day for the rest of my life.

I drove her to the brink then backed off. I lazily lapped on her clit 'til her moans were more than I could take. Her hands were now on my shoulders with her nails piercing my skin.

"Please, please," she pleaded.

"You ready for me?" I asked.

She nodded and tried to pull me up her body.

I slowly made my way up her body 'til my dick was pressing against her wet pussy.

"You sure you want this, Raven? We do this and everything is going to change."

I didn't want to stop. It would kill me if she told me to leave, but I wanted to be sure that this was what she wanted.

"Swear to God, Clash, if you don't fuck me within the next ten seconds, I am going to scream."

That's what I needed to hear.

Things were going to change. She knew it just as much as I did. But being with her was too strong of a pull to ignore.

I plunged inside her. The walls of her pussy contracting around me, and I growled deep. "Holy fuck."

"Yes," she gasped. Her arms wound around my neck, and she cocked her legs wide. "Fuck me, Clash."

I moved fast, hammering into her.

Her pleads and moans for more surrounded us.

My breathing was labored, and my balls tightened with each thrust.

Raven was the best pussy I had ever had.

Raven was just the best ever.

"Clash, God, please," she gasped. "I'm gonna come."

I hooked my hands in the crook of her knees and pressed them toward the bed. I lifted back and pounded into her.

Her eyes rolled back into her head, and she screamed my name. I watched her orgasm wash over her and knew that was something I would never get tired of seeing. Her pussy clamped down on my dick, and on the next thrust, I exploded inside her.

Her name ripped from my lips, and I collapsed on top of her.

Her arms wrapped around me, and our heavy breathing was the only sound in the room.

A few minutes later, we both finally caught our breath and her hands were tracing lazy circles on my back.

"That was not what I expected to happen when you walked in here."

"That a bad thing?" I muttered against her skin.

"It was a pleasant surprise I would like to do again."

I chuckled deep and rolled to the side. I gathered her in my arms and managed to pull the blanket over us. "Give me a quick twenty-minute nap and I'll be up for that. You wore me the hell out, beautiful."

"Same." She smothered a yawn with the back of her hand and sighed.

"One of us needs to turn the lights off."

"Siri," she called. "Turn off the lights."

The lights flickered off, and we were surrounded in darkness.

"You mean to tell me you can do that and I've been getting up every night to turn the lights off?" I grumbled.

If I would have known Raven had some fancy shit to turn the lights off, I totally would have used that instead of getting up all of the time.

She giggled and pressed a kiss to my shoulder. "I liked watching your backside every time you got up."

"I feel slightly used."

"I'll make it up to you later."

I slapped her ass. "You fucking better."

She settled into me, and her breathing evened out. "Twenty minutes," she mumbled sleepily.

It was longer than twenty minutes later, but I had that sweet pussy three more times before the sun came up.

I finally fell asleep with the sweet taste of her pussy on my lips, and I knew I was the luckiest bastard in the whole world.

*

Chapter Fifteen

Raven

"We need to talk." Wrecker's voice was low and even.

I closed my eyes and prayed to be anywhere but here.

"I stopped by your room last night but you must have been sleeping."

I grabbed a bottle of water and turned around to look at Wrecker. "Must have been."

Or I was about to have the best sex of my life. I had made the right choice to not answer the door for Wrecker last night.

It was only a little after seven, and I had left Clash in bed as I went to the kitchen to find something for my grumbling stomach.

"We don't need to talk, Wrecker."

I twisted the cap off the bottle and took a long drink. I never wanted to talk to him. At least, about this.

"Yeah, we do."

And since Wrecker thought it needed to happen, it was going to.

"Fine, talk."

He could talk all he wanted but it wasn't going to change anything.

He leaned against the kitchen counter and folded his arms across his chest. "I'm sorry."

"Okay, good talk."

He apologized. Time to move on. Though I wasn't sure what he was apologizing for.

I tried to make an escape past him, but he put his arm up and moved in my way.

"Got a lot of shit to say, Raven, and you're going to hear it even if you don't want to."

I rolled my eyes. "Then spit it out."

"I'm sorry I wasn't there when you needed me. I thought putting you in foster care would be the best thing for you. I didn't have a place to live or a steady job to support you with. I was crashing on my friends' couches and scraping by doing odd jobs here and there. I didn't even have my college diploma to help me get a better a job. I didn't have anything, Raven. How was I supposed to take care of you?"

"I was fifteen, Wrecker, not five. I could have helped. I would have gotten a job."

He shook his head. "That wasn't a responsibility I wanted to put on you."

"So instead, you thought putting me in foster care where I could get raped seemed like a better option over getting a job?" I set the water bottle down and clapped my hands. "That was the best decision ever, Wrecker. Stick me in foster care and don't check on me for years."

"I didn't know that was going to happen to you." He clenched his jaw. "If I would have known that was happening to you, I would have gotten you out of there."

"But how would you have known, Wrecker. You didn't call me. You didn't write me. You did nothing!"

"I called!" he shouted back. "I called your fucking house, and I talked to your foster mom. She said you were withdrawn and quiet but doing good. I talked to your social worker. They all told me you were fine. They said you were fine!"

I laughed flatly. "Oh yeah, I was totally fine being raped and hit. It was the best years of my life," I spit out.

"You didn't say anything. You didn't tell anyone. How was I supposed to know something was happening?"

I shook my head. "I don't know, Wrecker."

I hadn't told anyone. I had acted like it wasn't happening. For almost one year, Shane had raped me two to three times a week until he went away to college. The last four months I lived in foster care, I lived in fear of the weekends he would come home.

That all ended the day Shane's mom got a phone call. That phone call had changed my life.

Shane had died.

He had been on his way home and a semi had blown a stop light.

They had told Shane's mom he died on impact, and I couldn't help but feel joy in knowing the man who had tormented me for years had died instantly.

"Why didn't you tell me? Why didn't you find a way to get to me?" he demanded.

I shook my head and felt the sickness start to climb up my throat. "Tell you? How was I supposed to tell you when I had no fucking clue where the hell you were?"

"I was here. You knew I wouldn't leave Weston," he insisted.

"Right. I should have known you would leave me but *never* leave Weston." I rolled my eyes and slammed my bottle of water down on the counter. "You are not going to stand here and somehow make me feel like I'm the wrong one in all of this. You have the chance to keep our family together and instead, you chose this!" I spun in a slow circle.

"It was the wrong choice, Raven. I can't go back and change it."

"So I'm just supposed to accept it? Accept the fact my brother would rather be with his new family and not his actual family."

"You're here now, dammit. I'm trying to fix it now," he insisted.

I wiped my nose with the back of my hand. "Fix? This is you fixing it? You act like I'm a burden and make me feel like I'm just a nuisance."

"Well, your fucking attitude doesn't really fucking make things easier."

I placed a hand on my chest. "I'm sorry my attitude if making things hard for you. I'm sorry that you can't lord over me like all of the guys in this club. I'm sorry that I will call you on your shit."

I needed to get out of here. I couldn't stand here and have Wrecker blame this on me. I knew I wasn't the most pleasant person to be around, but he had to realize he was a big part in why.

I pushed my way past Wrecker. I was leaving.

"Where the fuck do you think you're going?" he thundered.

I grabbed Cora's keys off the counter. I had my phone in my pocket, and I ran for the door.

"Raven," he called.

I was out the door and hitting the unlock button on the keys before he moved. I swung the car door open and jammed the key into the ignition. The car roared to life, and I slammed it into reverse. Wrecker was in my rearview mirror when I pulled onto the road.

He was going to come after me. I knew that he wasn't going to just let me leave, but I needed some space to breath. I needed to not be in the clubhouse that was his. I needed to be away from him to think.

I just needed to think.

I passed the city limit sign for Weston, and thankfully, Wrecker wasn't behind me.

For a second, I was alone and I could finally fall apart.

*

Chapter Sixteen

Clash

"What the hell do you mean she's gone?"

Wrecker ran his fingers through his hair and paced the length of Raven's room. "I was just trying to talk to her. I've been wanting to talk to her for two weeks, and I can never get to her."

"And this is why I didn't want you to get to her. She wasn't ready to fucking listen to you."

I grabbed my pants off the floor and pulled them on.

Wrecker had knocked on the door and had thankfully given me enough time to pull my underwear on before he busted in. I had been surprised as hell when I had woken up and Raven wasn't in bed with me.

Now, I knew the reason why she was gone.

"We have to find her."

I pulled my shirt on and sat down on the bed to pull my socks and boots on. "We aren't doing anything. You're the whole fucking reason why she keeps running." I had no idea where the hell Raven would go. She barely knew Weston. "What was she wearing when she left?"

I finished lacing up my boots and grabbed my phone off her desk.

"Shirt and shorts. She didn't even have shoes on."

For Christ's sake.

"She took Cora's car?"

He nodded. "I was going to chase after her but I didn't want to push her away even more."

He had already done a bang up job at that.

"I'm out of here."

"I'm coming with you," he insisted.

I spun around and got in his face. "You're not doing anything. You're the fucking reason why Raven is the way she is. You really think that you chasing her down and dragging her back to the clubhouse is going to help?"

"What else am I supposed to do?" he yelled.

"Act like her fucking brother and not the President of a goddamn MC!" I roared. "She's your fucking family and you treat some stranger off the street better than her."

I looked around the room for my keys. I didn't have time to stand around and argue with Wrecker.

Raven was right. He wasn't going to see her side of things. At least, not now. I spotted my keys under a pile of her papers.

"What are you going to do?" he asked.

I shoved my keys in my pocket and grabbed my cut. "Find Raven."

"And bring her back here."

I shook my head. "Not making any promises, brother. This isn't about you and what you want."

I stormed out of the room and sent off a message to Raven.

She replied before I even threw my leg over my bike.

*

Chapter Seventeen

Raven

"Can I get you anything else?"

I shook my head. "I'm good."

The waitress looked at me for a beat then nodded. "I'll be over there if you need anything else."

I had driven until I saw the diner Clash and I had been to before. I was still in Weston, but at least I wasn't trapped in the clubhouse. "Thank you."

The waitress was giving off some serious motherly vibes.

"Can I get a coffee and a menu?" Clash stood behind the waitress and slid into the booth across from me.

"Oh, you were waiting for someone."

I slid my menu to Clash and sat back in the booth. "Yup."

She filled Clash's cup, and he looked the menu over.

He rattled off his order than looked at me. "You order anything?" he asked me.

I bit my lip and shook my head. While I had been smart enough to grab Cora's keys to make my getaway, I had failed to take any money with me.

"Double what I ordered and keep the coffee coming." He handed the waitress the menu, and she nodded.

I waited 'til the waitress was gone before I relaxed. "Pretty sure she was about to sit down with me before you came. Thank you for saving me."

Clash chuckled and took a sip of his coffee. "Glad to be of service, beautiful."

"I'm assuming we need to talk."

"If that's what you want to do."

I tilted my head to the side. "I get a choice?"

"You always have a choice, beautiful. We could talk about what happened between you and Wrecker, or the stock market."

I wrinkled my nose. "I know absolutely nothing about the stock market."

"Thank God," Clash laughed. "Neither do I. Not exactly on the life path for knowing the stock market."

I laid my head back on the booth and sighed. "I don't know how to handle Wrecker, Clash."

"Most don't."

"So what am I supposed to do?"

"What did you do before he asked you to help with The Ultra?"

I laughed and shook my head. "Worked as a bartender."

"That's it?" he asked.

I nodded. "Yup. I was most definitely a loner. The only reason I became friends with Mayra was because of working for The Ultra." A smile spread across my lips. "I don't know why but people don't really approach me."

"Maybe it's the giant chip on your shoulder and the nose ring?"

I touched the small hoop in my nose. "I like my nose ring."

"I do too, beautiful. I just think it might add to the vibe you put off."

I loved my nose ring. I had gotten it the day I turned eighteen and had never taken it out. How could he say people didn't talk to me because of it? Next, he was going to tell me my hair and tattoos was part of the problem, too.

"What vibe are you talking about?" I asked.

"When I first met you, I thought you were going to rip my balls off and shove them down my throat."

"You didn't even talk to me, Clash. Why would you think that?"

He chuckled and shook his head. "I didn't talk to you because I thought you were going to rip my balls off and shove them down my throat."

I rolled my eyes. "Can we move onto something else to talk about? Perhaps talking about the stock market?" I suggested sweetly.

"Or we can get back to Wrecker. You don't need to forgive him, Raven, but you need to move past it."

"Move past the fact he only thought about himself and not me?"

He nodded. "Yeah. That was ten years ago, and a shit-ton has happened since then."

"And how do I move on without forgiving him?"

I didn't want to be pissed off at Wrecker for the rest of my life, but I didn't know how to not be mad. He preached about brotherhood and having everyone's back, but he didn't have mine. He never had. Our parents died, and he just took off.

"Try to see it from his side."

I opened my mouth to protest, but Clash silenced me with a look.

"Just see it from his side. That doesn't mean you have to agree with his side. There are always two sides to the story, Raven."

I sighed. "Fine. I'll try to see it from his side. Then what?"

"Then you get on with your life and make sure shit like that never happens again. You've gotten through so much, Raven, but you still have all of it weighing you down." He looked around and leaned close. "I do have one question."

"Oh, Lord. Hit me with it," I muttered.

"The guy. What happened to him? Did anything ever happen to him?"

"He's dead, Clash."

His eyes connected with mine. "Dead?"

"Yes, and before you start to think I did it, I didn't," I laughed. "He was on his way home from college and got into a car accident. He died on impact."

"Now that's what I call karma." He cleared his throat. "Though, I gotta admit I was kind of hoping to be the one to rain karma down on him."

I fanned my face and swooned. "And they say chivalry is dead."

"You're such a smartass, Raven. I think you need your ass paddled."

This time, I really did swoon, and my cheeks heated. "Is that a threat or a promise?"

"You'll have to just wait and find out."

The waitress brought our breakfast over, and we ate in silence while I tried to focus on my food and not what he had said.

Clash pushed his finished plate away. "So what are you thinking you're going to do now? You already committed grand theft auto today, and it's only eight thirty in the morning. We've got the whole day in front of us."

"I had the keys. I did not commit grand theft auto." I finished my bacon and licked my fingers. "And, for the record, it wouldn't be grand theft auto. I did not take that car by force and sell it."

"The fact you know that makes me wonder *why* you would know that."

I eyed him knowingly. "Like you didn't know that."

"I plead the fifth, beautiful. Only a fool brags about the stupid things he's done."

Clash signaled for the check, and I suddenly realized I had no idea what we were going to do. I had a pile of work, but I didn't want to go back to the clubhouse.

"What are we going to do?"

"First, we're gonna take Cora's car back to her."

"And then?"

The waitress dropped off the check, and Clash dropped some money on top of it.

"Then, I know you probably got some work to do so there are a couple of options on how you can get that done."

I took a sip of my water and wondered if we could just stay at the diner all day. "I'm listening."

"We go back to the clubhouse and you work there."

I wrinkled my nose. I normally wasn't one to run away from my problems, but I just wasn't ready to talk to Wrecker. "Option two, please."

A devilish grin spread across his lips. "We rent a room from the Stargazer Inn and see how much work you can get done there."

"Work? Are we talking about the same kind of work here? I think the only place I'll be able to actually work is at the library or a busy coffee shop."

In those two places, at least I would be able to keep my hands off Clash.

Clash leaned forward and grabbed my hand. "But what would be the fun in that?"

I rolled my eyes. "As much as I love your way of thinking, I do need to make some money to help pay for the house I just bought."

"Would one day of fun really hurt?" His thumb glided over the smooth skin of my palm.

Would one day really matter? I was basically caught up on everything, but I hated the idea of getting behind.

"Let's make a deal."

"I'm listening, beautiful."

"We take the car back, we pack a bag, and go to the library."

His brow furrowed. "You had me until the library."

I laughed and pulled my hand from his. "You let me work for a few hours at the library and then we can see if there are any vacancies at the Stargazer."

"We both get what we want?"

I nodded, slipped out of the booth, and winked at him over my shoulder. "I'll meet you back at the clubhouse, warden."

I heard him groan at the name, and I couldn't help but smile.

Clash may have me in his bed, but I was still going to keep him on his toes.

*

Chapter Eighteen

Clash

Bored.

So fucking bored.

We had been at the public library for five hours, and I was about to lose my mind.

I had flashbacks to grade school when we had walked through the doors. The first hour was okay. Raven talked to me, and we joked back and forth about all the trouble we got into in school.

Now we were entering the sixth hour of being here and something was going to have to happen to keep me awake.

Raven and I were the only ones here besides the two librarians who hadn't left the front desk the whole time we had been here. Apparently, the Weston library was not a happening place on a Thursday afternoon.

When we had gotten back to the clubhouse Wrecker's bike was gone, and the only member around was Freak. Raven had been relieved we were able to grab everything we needed and get out of there without talking to Wrecker.

I reminded her she was eventually going to have to clear the air with him, but she wasn't interested in worrying about that.

"Raven," I whispered.

She looked up from her computer screen and blinks slowly. "Uh, yeah?"

An idea had just popped into my head, and I was too bored to realize it might be a bad idea. "I'm gonna go look around."

"'Kay." She turned her eyes back to her screen, and I shoved my phone into my pocket.

I did a couple laps of the place trying to find the most secluded area and wound up in the historical section in the back corner three rows away from where Raven and I had been sitting.

Help.

I stared at my phone 'til Raven replied.

Uh, what?

Need your help. Head to the back corner.

I waited five minutes before I heard footsteps approaching.

"Clash?" she whispered.

I peeked around the corner of the row I was in and waved Raven to me.

"What are you doing?" she laughed.

I pulled her into my arms and pressed her against the stack of books. "Needed a break," I whispered.

"You're crazy," she giggled.

I pressed a finger to her lips and shook my head. "Shh, beautiful. No one can hear us."

"What are you thinking?" she asked softly.

"I was sitting there trying to remember what your lips felt like wrapped around my dick but I couldn't quite remember."

She rolled her eyes. "It happened last night. If you can't remember then we better stop and get some ginkgo biloba for your memory."

"No fucking clue what that is. Is it like Viagra?"

She slapped me on the chest and laughed. "No," she hissed.

"Good. I don't need that shit yet. All I need is you and I'm good to go." My lips drifted over her neck and placed random kisses.

"What are you doing, Clash?"

"I told you."

She wrapped her arms around my neck and tipped her head to the side to give me better access. "So you want me to give you head in the library?"

I pressed my lips to her ear. "When you say it like that, I feel like I'm back in high school trying to get to second base."

"I think you have a lot more game than you did back in high school."

"You're probably right. There's no way in hell I would have been able to get a hot piece of ass like yours back then."

"Oh, please," she whispered. "I bet you had all of the girls chasing after you."

My hands traveled down her body and around to her ass. "None like you, beautiful. Never had anyone like you."

She laid a finger to my lips. "Keep talking and a lot more is going to happen than a blow job."

She dropped to her knees, and her fingers popped open the button on my pants.

The fantasy of every high school boy was about to happen to me. A blow job in between the stacks of books in the library.

Raven tugged down the zipper of my jeans and pulled my pants and underwear down until my dick bobbed out. Her hand wrapped around the shaft, and she spit on my dick as she stroked up and down.

My heart felt like it was about to beat out of my chest, and my breathing was short and shallow.

Her mouth wrapped around my dick, and I watched her head bob up and down on me.

"Holy fuck," I gasped.

She tapped her fingers against my thigh and gently shook her head.

Here I thought she was going to be the loud one, and I was the one who couldn't keep my mouth shut.

I threaded my fingers through her hair and controlled the speed. She moaned as I pulled her hair and tipped her head back to look up at me.

My dick slid in and out of her mouth, and I watched every second of it.

"That fucking mouth is mine," I whispered harshly.

Her eyes heated with desire, and her hand on my thigh tightened. She slid my dick down her throat further than she had before and gagged slightly. Her eyes watered, and she backed off.

"Mother fucking shit," I moaned.

The feel of her throat tightening against my dick was fucking heaven.

She pulled off my dick and wiped her mouth with the back of her hand. "Again," she whispered.

Her mouth was back on my dick before I could ask what she meant. Again, she took me deep but this time, she relaxed her throat and didn't gag. She continued to take me deep and suck hard with each pull up. Her head bobbed faster, and her hand on my shaft slid down to my balls.

She rolled and tugged my balls, and my head lolled back. I was ready to blow my load straight down her throat. She doubled her efforts, sensing I was close to coming. Her hand moved faster. Her mouth sucked harder.

My balls tightened in her hand, and a low moan escaped my lips.

Cum spurted from my dick, and she drank down every last drop. Even when I didn't have any more to give, she lazily sucked on my dick with her eyes locked on mine.

She pulled her head back 'til my dick fell from her mouth and her hand continued to stroke me. "That was nice," she whispered.

She tucked me back into my boxers, pulled up my pants, and buttoned them.

I was too spent to even help her.

She stood and wiped the corner of her mouth with her finger. "I think we've done everything we can here today."

I pushed her up against the shelf behind her and pressed my lips to hers. She moaned into the kiss, and I delved my fingers back into her hair.

She just drained my dick but that little move of wiping her mouth already had me hard again, and this time, I wanted her pussy.

"Pack your shit and let's go," I ordered against her lips.

"Sure thing, warden," she whispered. She pressed a swift kiss to my lips. "It's my turn when we get to the hotel." She winked and slipped from my arms. She strutted away and glanced at me over her shoulder. "Don't keep me waiting."

She disappeared from sight, and I tipped my head back. I closed my eyes and repeated the alphabet backward in my head until my dick went down and my hands weren't clenched at my sides.

Raven was the hottest chick I had ever been with, and I wasn't going to let her go.

Hopefully, she felt the same way and I wasn't just something to help pass the time 'til she got away from the club.

*

Chapter Nineteen

Raven

"How much would it cost to rent this place until I can move into my house?"

Clash pulled his shirt over his head and sat down on the bed. "Weren't you the one who said you needed to work your ass off to pay for said house? I'm pretty sure paying for a hotel room for a month would probably tap into all of that money you need for the house." He pulled on his boots and turned to look at me. "Though I have to say, I do like the hotel better than your room at the clubhouse. A much smaller chance of Wrecker knocking on the door while I'm trying to give you the D."

I rolled my eyes and hitched my computer bag over my shoulder. "Who would have thought you would be the voice of reason?"

He shrugged. "I'm just as surprised at it as you."

He grabbed his cut off the back of the chair and pulled it on.

"You really do wear that all of the time, don't you?"

"It's part of who I am, beautiful."

Yesterday, we had gotten to the hotel and hadn't surfaced from bed until we were both exhausted and needed sustenance. A large pizza and breadsticks were ordered and then we were back at it for rounds three and four before the sun rose.

We had slept until noon, and as much as I wanted to never return to the clubhouse and see Wrecker, that was exactly what we were doing.

"Do you have actual family?"

"Yeah, beautiful. My mom and dad are still alive."

That was surprising to me. I had always thought the guys in clubs were a bunch of misfits who didn't have much in the way of family and were looking for a brotherhood like Wrecker had.

"Then why are you part of the club?"

He tipped his head to the side. "Because I like knowing I belong to something. These guys are my brothers and will have my back, no matter what."

"What do your parents think about it?"

Before my mom and dad had passed away, I had to think they wouldn't be so accepting of Wrecker being the president of an MC.

"They're good with it." He grabbed his keys off the dresser and the duffel bag off the floor.

"That's it? They're just good with it?" I laughed. "Do they really get what the Fallen Lords is?"

Clash laughed. "I think they've seen a few episodes of *Sons of Anarchy*." Mom asked me if we had a guy like Chucky."

"She didn't," I laughed.

"She sure did." Clash dropped his sunglasses over his eyes and moved to the door. "She doesn't believe me so I plan on having her and Dad come out to the club sometime. That's the only way she is ever going to believe, if she sees it for herself."

He opened the door and motioned for me to go out.

"You have just completely blown my mind. I have no idea what your parents are actually like, but all I picture is your everyday average Midwest couple that really has no idea what an MC is."

Clash shrugged. "That's about right. My dad is an engineer and my mom works at the local bakery."

"They live here?"

"Nah. About an hour away. I try to visit when I can. That's where I was about a month ago when Freak kept an eye on you." He hitched his thumb toward the parking lot. "Let's get a move on it, beautiful. I don't want to hear later how you didn't get any work done because I distracted you all day."

I glanced around the hotel room to make sure we had everything. "You always seem to distract me," I mumbled.

"You know you like it."

I slid my sunglasses onto my face and walked out of the room. I did like it. That was part of the problem. I could have a mountain to work to do, and all Clash had to do was look at me and I would be next to him in a heartbeat.

Clash had taken the time to get to know me and to understand me. I never had someone like that in my life before.

I liked it so much, I was absolutely terrified I was going to lose it.

Clash stashed everything in the saddle bags of the bike, and I climbed on behind him.

He glanced over his shoulder at me before he started the engine. "You done running, beautiful?"

I knew what he was talking about.

I knew he was right about everything he had said about Wrecker and me.

The problem I had was actually accepting it and moving on.

"I think so, but if I do run, will you chase me again?"

"As long as you let me."

"I guess I'll just take you with me the next time I run," I whispered.

"Now that is something I can get behind."

I leaned forward and pressed a kiss to his lips. "Take me back to my home for the next month, warden," I whispered.

Clash nodded and cranked up the bike.

I could take another month living in the Fallen Lords Clubhouse.

It was what would happen to Clash and me after I moved out I was worried about. He was with me now because I was plopped down in the middle of his world.

What would happen when I wasn't in the room right next to him?

Would he really still want me, or were we playing with borrowed time?

*

Chapter Twenty

Clash

"Where were you?"

Brinks was leaning against his door once again, shirtless and looking like he had just rolled out of bed.

"What the fuck are you doing here?" Last I knew, Brinks was in River Valley indefinitely so he could keep an eye on Jenkins.

"Shit is so fucked up in River Valley. I was there for a week and never saw Jenkins. It was like the guy had fucking disappeared."

"That's fucking fishy." That wasn't good at all. "You go by the clubhouse?"

"Did. The three guys that were still part of the club were basically packing up their shit and getting out of dodge. It appears that the original Fallen Lords MC chapter is no more." Clash nodded toward Raven's door. "It appears while I was gone things changed with the pissed off one."

I glanced at her door. "She's not really the pissed off one anymore. At least, not with me anymore."

"That's surprising as hell."

It was. Raven still had some shit she had to work through, but I wanted to be the one there for her while she figured it out.

"Not saying she isn't sassy as fuck anymore, but I get her now."

"Guess that's all any relationship really is."

I glanced at Brinks. "What the hell are you doing looking like you just rolled out of bed?"

It was four o'clock in the afternoon. I was all for sleeping in but four was a little bit ridiculous.

A shit-eating grin spread across his lips. "I did just get out of bed but I wasn't sleeping."

"You dog," I laughed.

"A man has needs, brother." He hitched his thumb over his shoulder. "And that woman knows how to satisfy each and every one of them."

"You're gonna be the exception, aren't you? Finding your chick without having her needing saving or some bullshit."

Brinks chuckled. "Everyone needs saving, Clash. It's just that sometimes the only person who can save them is themselves."

That was sort of what Raven was. I was there for her, but for her to actually move on and become happy, she was going to have to be the one to make those changes.

"That's pretty fucking accurate."

Brinks nodded and ducked back into his room. I tried to sneak a peek into his room but he blocked my view and closed the door.

"You think you could have grabbed your beer?" Raven walked up to me and pressed my open beer into my chest. "Honestly, man," she scoffed.

I grabbed her around the waist and pulled her close. "You always gonna call me on my shit?"

"It seems like someone needs to do it, so it might as well be me."

My phone buzzed in my pocket, and Raven pulled it out. She wrinkled her nose and held it up for me to read.

"My brother beckons you."

"Figured that was coming."

With shit going sideways with Jenkins, I figured it was only a matter of time before Wrecker called a meeting.

"You know I want to know what is going on, but I know you can't tell me, so I'm going to work on a new design job and not think about how bullshitty it is that I can't know what you know."

"That was a lot of knowing," I laughed.

"Not really since I don't know what you know." She tried to keep a straight face but her lips curled up into a smile. "Maybe Alice put a bit too much Malibu in my drink."

"I think that might be a good assumption, beautiful."

After we had gotten home from the hotel, Raven worked for a few hours before Alice knocked and announced that she was ordering Mexican food and our attendance was mandatory.

While Wrecker was there, he had kept his distance from Raven. I think he finally got that he couldn't come at her like a fucking freight train and roll right over her.

Alice had ordered a fuck-ton of tacos, fajitas, rice, beans, and nachos, and she thought the perfect accompaniment to all of that was Malibu and pineapple cocktails.

"It just tasted like Hawaii though."

"Hawaii?" I chuckled. Raven was definitely tipsy. "Maybe you should just take a nap while I'm in my meeting."

She pressed her finger to my lips. "That might be better than me trying to design a logo for a florist."

I pressed a kiss to the pad of her finger. "Probably. It's early enough that you can sleep it off for a bit and work on the logo later."

"So smart," she slurred.

I helped Raven into bed and turned on a movie before heading to the meeting. Raven's eyelids were fluttering shut before I walked out of the room, and I knew she would be snoring by the time I was two feet from the door.

Almost everyone was sitting around the table when I walked in. "Brinks behind you?" Nickel asked.

I shook my head. "Nah. I did see him right before you texted. He's gotta get dressed so I'm sure he's on the way."

"What the hell do you mean he had to get dressed?" Pipe asked.

I sat down in my chair and shrugged. This had nothing to do with me. If Brinks wanted to tell everyone he was banging some chick, he could be the one to do it.

"Think you could give a little bit more notice?" Brinks grumbled. He skidded into the room and plopped down next to me.

"I'm sorry. Did club business interrupt your reunion with whatever chick you're banging now?" Wrecker growled.

Brinks glared at Wrecker, but he didn't say anything.

"Where's the gavel?" Freak asked.

Everyone looked at him.

"That your main concern?" Slayer laughed.

Freak shrugged. "I just liked it the last time."

"I'll take note of the fact Freak would like the gavel for the next meeting," Pipe snickered.

Wrecker slammed his fist down on the table.

"How's that for you?" Boink whispered to Freak. "No gavel, but you get Wrecker's fist of pissedoffness."

"Can you fucking idiots shut the hell up?" Wrecker thundered.

We all sobered and shut out mouths.

"As you can see, Brinks and Freak are back from River Valley. It seems Jenkins took off, and no one knows where the hell he went."

"Good riddance," Maniac put in.

"It would be good if we knew for a fact that he wasn't going to come back." Wrecker sat back in his chair and folded his arms over his chest. "The thing with Jenkins is, I knew he's not the type to disappear. He's planning something. This happening makes sense with the rumblings I've heard about him. He's trying to find allies and come back bigger."

"No one is going to fucking work with Jenkins. Everyone within a four state radius knows he's not someone you want to hitch your wagon to." Nickel shook his head. "He was the reason I almost left the fucking club a couple of years ago."

"He was the reason we all almost left," Brinks muttered.

"No one established will work with Jenkins, but it's the new guys who are coming up in the muling and drug game that will be looking for a partner to help them. Jenkins maybe a fucking idiot, but he does know how shit works." Wrecker pulled out his phone. "There are two new guys who are cooking in Ohio that are rumored to be looking for partners. Del Rink and Tray Bein."

"Never fucking heard of them. You really think we need to worry about this? We're fucking cuddled up with The Ultra and are buddies with the Banachi's." Slayer bumped fists with Maniac. "I mean, come on. We're basically the fucking kings right now."

"And Jenkins used to be the king. He wants that back. He'll do anything and that's what makes him dangerous." Wrecker dropped his phone on the table.

Slayer dropped his chin to his chest. "Let me guess. Two of us are being sent to bumfuck Ohio to keep an eye on these newbie idiots."

"No."

Slayer's head snapped up and his jaw dropped. "You're fucking kidding me."

Wrecker shook his head. "Jenkins is going to come after us. We don't know where he is, but I know here, on our turf, this is where we are the strongest."

"So, he's coming, and we're just going to wait?" Brinks steepled his fingers in front of him. "So, while we wait, we get stronger."

Wrecker pointed at Brinks. "Right on. But there is also something we have that Jenkins might want."

"Cora."

We all looked at Freak.

"And that is why we patched you in." Wrecker looked at Freak with approval. "He hasn't shown any interest in Cora before, but I feel with him having basically no one with him that he might remember he has a sister."

"So, we use her as bait?" I asked.

Brinks stirred next to me. "We're really gonna use Cora to draw Jenkins in? That seems a bit stupid."

I glanced over at him and saw he looked fucking tense. Brinks never looked tense. He always just went with the flow and figured shit out as it came at him.

"We're not going to dangle her like a fucking carrot in front of him, but we have to realize he might come for her."

"Not fucking it!" Slayer shouted. "I am not keeping an eye on that woman. I managed to dodge having to watch Raven and I would like to continue my streak of not having to deal with the women."

"Your day will come," Pipe laughed.

"No fucking way." Slayer shook his head. "I do not need some ol' lady coming in and telling me what to do and where to do it. No way, no fucking how."

Wrecker laughed and shook his head. "I wait for the day that you actually settle down, Slayer. Might not be for another ten fucking years, but I know that shit is going to happen."

"We keep doing what we're doing and wait for shit to hit the fan?" Boink cleared his throat. "That's it?"

Wrecker nodded. "We stay vigilant and keep an ear to the ground. Ninety-nine percent of the time, there are always rumblings before shit goes down. I know with Jenkins, he won't be able to move without everyone knowing what he is doing."

"But he's disappeared without anyone knowing where he went," Brinks pointed out. "You can't really say we know what this guy is going to do."

"And that's why we're not going to do anything." Wrecker sighed. "Look, we're doing nothing but keeping our eyes wide open because we know something is coming."

"After this, I'd love to keep our eyes closed and just enjoy our women."

Pipe pointed at Nickel. "That is the best idea I've heard in years."

"That may happen, brothers. This might be nothing. But this might also be the hardest fight we'll have." Wrecker slammed his hand on the table. "Let's just be prepared for whatever it is."

*

Raven

I hummed under my breath and relaxed into the wall of warmth next to me.

"You really gonna stay asleep?"

Clash was in bed with me, and as much as I liked having him there, I just wanted to sleep.

"Sleep is good." I snuggled into his chest. "It's even better when you're sleeping with me."

"I thought maybe we could do a little bit more than sleeping," he suggested. His voice was low and rough, and I could tell he was really wanting more than sleep.

"Raincheck, warden."

"You serious right now?"

I had never been more serious in all of my life. It felt like I hadn't slept in ten years, and all I wanted to do was pass out and not surface for a good day or two.

"Blame Alice," I mumbled. "I got a full tummy and fuzzy Malibu brain."

"All right, woman. Just know, your ass is mine in the morning."

"Sounds like fun." I reached up and pressed a finger to his lips. "Now, *shh* and let me sleep."

"Siri, turn off the lights," Clash rumbled. He pulled the blanket over us and sighed. "Sleep, beautiful."

That was something I was going to have no problem doing. I should have woken the hell up and asked him how his meeting was, but I couldn't find the words, and I was too relaxed to even act like I cared.

I'd add that to the list of things I was going to do when I woke up. Right after Clash cashed in his raincheck.

*

Chapter Twenty-One

Clash

"Stay just like that."

"Clash," Raven gasped. "Please."

Raven was on her knees, her face pushed into her pillow, and my dick was buried deep inside her.

"Tell me what you want, beautiful."

My hands gripped her hips, and I knew if I moved them, she would collapse onto the bed. Raven was seconds away from coming, and I knew I wasn't too far behind either.

"You, Clash. I want you."

I thrust hard and deep, and she fell apart beneath me. My balls tightened, and I emptied my load into her sweet pussy.

"Holy moly," she gasped.

I collapsed next to her and pulled her into my arms. "Holy moly is right. Pretty sure the whole clubhouse heard you come."

"I don't even have the energy to be upset about that," she mumbled.

Once she came down from the high she was on, I was pretty sure she was going to care.

"That's what happens when you decide to sleep and not let me fuck you," I grumbled.

"I'm not even mad about that. I might have to make you wait sometimes if that is how you're gonna do me." Her breathing evened out, and I thought she was asleep again. "How was your meeting?"

"Raincheck," I mumbled. It had worked for her last night when I wanted something and she didn't.

"That ain't gonna work," she laughed. "Tell me about your meeting. What craziness is coming for the Fallen Lords now?"

Meetings were only called out of the blue when shit was going down.

"We don't know what is coming."

She cracked open one eye. "Wrecker called a meeting to tell you guys something is coming but he doesn't know what?"

"Basically. Though he's not even one hundred percent sure something even is coming."

"It sounds like he called a meeting just to call a meeting."

I chuckled and pressed a kiss to her cheek. "It does sound that way, but as much as you have a problem with anything your brother does, he knows what he's talking about. A guy we messed with a year or so ago might be coming for the Lords but we don't know because he's ghosted."

She opened both of her eyes, and I was mesmerized by her beauty. If I was going to wake up to Raven every day for the rest of my life, it wouldn't be enough. I was going to need ten lifetimes of waking up with her for it to be even close enough time with her.

"You need to stop messing with assholes." A huge smile spread across her lips. "I should totally be president of the Fallen Lords. We'd keep to ourselves, ride Harleys, and eat pizza."

"In that order?" I chuckled.

She closed her eyes and sighed contently. "Exactly in that order."

"Sounds like you should be a part of the Girl Gang. You guys all think being in an MC is easy as riding a Harley."

"It is," she muttered. "You guys muck it up by thinking too much."

I smacked her ass. "We're gonna have to agree to disagree with that one, beautiful. Imagine having another Girl Gang move into Weston. Now there are two Girl Gangs in the same territory. What would you do?"

"Join forces and take over the world," she muttered.

A light knock sounded on the door. "Raven. Are you up?"

"Which one of your chicks is that?" I asked.

"Mayra," Raven croaked. "What do you want?" she shouted.

"We're going bowling in two hours. You in?"

The girls had talked about getting together to go bowling a few weeks ago, and they were finally getting their asses in gear to plan it. "Are we in?" she whispered.

"If you wanna go, we can go."

"Count us in," Raven hollered.

"Sweet!" Mayra yelled. "Meet in the common room when you're ready. I think Karmen and Nikki are planning to pregame."

"10-4." Raven laid her head back down and sighed. "I need to shower and try to look pretty."

"That doesn't take much."

She put her hand on my face and pushed. "No," she moaned. "I can't take your random sweetness right now. We do not have time to have sex again."

We did have time to do it again. It just wasn't going to happen in the bed. It was time to cross off another place I wanted to have sex with Raven.

"Hop in the shower and I'll help wash your back."

She studied my face knowingly. "You're gonna fuck me in the shower, aren't you?"

"You'll have to get your ass in there and find out."

She grumbled under breath and rolled out of bed. "You're damn near insatiable."

"Only for you, beautiful."

"Keep it that way." She grabbed a pair of panties from her drawer and walked into the bathroom. "Get your ass in here", she called. "I'm not about to be fucked in a cold shower."

I tossed back the covers and walked into the bathroom bare-assed naked. I was fucking insatiable when it came to Raven. I had just fucked her, and I was already hard for her again.

Life was pretty fucking good right now, and there wasn't a damn thing I would change about it.

*

Raven

"What's that say?" My blurred vision was making this hard.

"Which one?"

"Mine," I muttered.

Mayra squinted up at the screen. "Uh, I think that is a twenty-nine."

I blinked rapidly. "We're in the ninth frame?"

Mayra snorted and smothered her laugh with the back of her hand. "Uh, yeah. But you can totally come back in the tenth frame."

I sat back and folded my arms over my chest. "Yeah, sure. I can totally get three strikes in a row and beat you all."

Mayra giggled and took a sip of her beer. "You're really not that far behind."

"Mayra," I grumbled. "The lowest score out of the seven of us besides mine is ninety-eight. Do you know how to do math? It's a good thing Wren is the secretary of the club and in charge of the money."

"We don't have money," she hiccupped.

"Well, whatever. You should probably let Boink know that you suck at math and he better take care of the checkbook when you two get hitched."

She giggled and set her glasses down. "He already knows."

"You're up, Raven. Try to hit the pins this time and not the gutter."

I flipped off Cora and grabbed my ball from the ball return. "I'm still warming up," I muttered.

"Right," she drawled. "It normally takes three games for someone to warm up." She sat down next to Mayra and pointed to the pins at the end of our lane. "Look at the pins when you throw the ball, not the fucking floor."

"I don't look at the floor," I muttered.

I totally did. She had been telling me the past two hours while we bowled that I needed to put my hips into it and keep my eye on the pins. I hadn't listened to either thing.

"The guys are done. They bowled five games." Karmen leaned against the podium type thing that had our computer thingy that controlled our lane.

I really had no idea what any of this bowling stuff was called. I was mostly here to drink beer and eat nachos. Both of which I was good at. Bowling, not so much.

I flung the ball down the lane two more times and only managed to hit one pin.

"At least it's an even number," Alice pointed out.

"That's one way to put a positive spin on it," I laughed. I sat down and toed off my shoes. "I'm done. You guys can keep going, but I can only suck for so long before I need to throw the towel in."

We had paid for two hours of bowling and that was about ninety minutes longer than I wanted to bowl.

"You can pick the group activity next time, Raven." Nikki grabbed her ball from the return. "Mini golf maybe?"

I shook my head. "I'm thinking more of a movie outing or dinner. Neither of those things we have to keep score." I spotted Clash by the bar and grabbed my empty glass. "You guys need refills?" A chorus of "yes" rang out. "You guys keep bowling and I'll be back with refreshments."

Clash was sitting at the bar next to Wrecker, and they had their heads bowed to each other as they talked.

I leaned against the bar and waited for the bartender to come over. "Three fuzzy nipples, a purple dragon, and three tequila sunrises."

"Those actual drinks or did you just make all that up?"

I smiled at Boink. "I'm not too sure about the first two, but I'm positive the last one is an actual drink. I think Karmen and Nikki might have made up the first two."

Nickel was sitting on the stool next to me with his back to the bar and his eyes on Karmen. "Karmen is well on her way to being a pirate, I see."

"Karmen the pirate," I laughed.

Nickel chuckled. "Yup. You get rum in her, and she thinks she's ready to set sail with Johnny Depp and saying aye every other word."

"I don't think she was quite there yet."

Nickel nodded to the drinks the bartender was lining up on the bar. "Won't be long until she is." Nickel wandered over to Karmen and wrapped his arms around her.

I also ordered another platter of nachos and mozzarella sticks. It was a night of bowling, drinking, and junk food.

"Having fun, beautiful?" Clash called from a few barstools away.

"I got a thirty the last game."

Clash cringed. "Maybe you just need to get warmed up?"

I laughed and shook my head. "Nah. I think I just realized I'm not much of an athlete. I'm more of a team supporter and good drink orderer."

Wrecker chuckled. "You sound just like Mom."

I looked at Wrecker. That was the first time he had ever mentioned Mom to me since she died. Hell, that was basically the first time he had talked to me since I stormed out of the club. It was like we had both been avoiding each other.

"Mama really wasn't much of an athlete, was she?" I said softly.

Wrecker shook his head. "She sure the hell wasn't."

A ruckus broke out at the other end of the bar, and Slayer hollered for Clash to come settle an argument for them.

"Behave," Clash mumbled as he walked by me. "If you make a run for it, make sure you grab me."

He pressed a kiss to my cheek and gave my ass a squeeze.

"You seem happy, Raven."

I looked over at Wrecker. His eyes were studying me, and I fidgeted under his gaze.

"I'm good."

Wrecker picked at the label on his beer bottle. "I know now isn't the time to talk, but I want you to know I'm sorry."

His tone was even, and for the first time, it really felt like he meant it.

"I should have fought for you more. If I had known something like that would have happened to you, I would have moved heaven and earth to get you with me." He drained his beer and slammed the bottle down on the bar.

Tears clouded my eyes, and I stared down at the bar to keep them at bay. "I know you couldn't have known that was going to happen to me, Wrecker. I don't blame you for that."

"You sure do hate me, though," he said softly.

I looked up at him. "I did. I hated you something fierce. You chose a group of guys who you barely knew over me. You didn't call. You didn't come see me. You didn't care."

Now it was Wrecker's turn to look at the bar. "I did. I did all of that, Raven." He closed his eyes and shook his head. "I'd love to go back and do it all over again. I'd be the brother you deserved. I wouldn't leave you to take care of yourself when you were so young. I would have made sure you were safe. I cared about you but I didn't know how to show it."

"Thank you."

He wasn't trying to give me reasons why he did what he did. He wasn't justifying picking the club over me. He was sorry for what he did, and while it didn't change anything that had happened, it was going to change what was going to happen in the future.

"I want you to know that no one knows about what happened to you. Not that I don't want them to know I had a hand in that happening to you, but because it's yours to tell or not tell."

"Not even Alice?" I asked.

He shook his head. "As far as she knows, she thinks you're just a bitch."

I gasped then threw my head back laughing. "You would tell her that."

He shrugged and signaled to the bartender for another beer. "If she thought it was something else, she would bug the shit out of you 'til you told her what was wrong."

The bartender finished my drinks then set down Wrecker's beer in front of him. Wrecker moved closer and grabbed four of the drinks.

"There is something you should know, though."

I looked up at Wrecker, and for the first time in over ten years, I looked at him like he was my brother and not someone who had left me behind.

193

"If you ever need to talk to someone, Wren might be good. She went through something like you did. I don't know where your head is at when it comes to what happened to you, but I know she would talk if you needed it."

I nodded and grabbed the three other drinks. "Right now, I'm okay. I guess I dealt with that a lot better than I did losing you."

The couple of years after Shane died, I beat myself up pretty bad. I was lost and unsure of what I was supposed to feel. While I knew I shouldn't be mad someone had died, I knew that Shane dying was justice being served to him.

"Just one more thing and then we can put this brotherly talk behind us."

What else was there for Wrecker to say?

"I'm kind of afraid what this is going to be about."

Wrecker leaned close. "I know that you and Clash are together. I get it. I'm good with it. He seems to know how to handle you better than anyone."

"Wrecker, please stop." I did not want to talk about whatever was happening with Clash and I with him.

"Just know if anything ever happens to you, you come first to me. I'll kick his ass in a heartbeat, and he'll be out on his ass."

I laughed and shook my head. "You don't need to do that, Wrecker. As hard as it was for me to finally get, I understand what this club means you. I get all of this."

I didn't know when it had happened, but I started understanding what all of this is. I saw the benefits of having people in your corner no matter what.

"I just want you to know even when you move out that all of this will be here for you."

I blinked slowly. "Move out?"

How did Wrecker know about that? I hadn't told anyone but Clash.

Clash.

He had been the one to tell Wrecker.

He had talked about me to Wrecker.

I didn't know why, but I felt the burn of betrayal move through me. I hadn't expected Clash to run to my brother and tell him what I was doing.

But when I thought about it, it made sense. Clash had a sort of loyalty to me, but I knew that his ultimately his loyalty was to the Fallen Lords.

I wasn't a part of the Fallen Lords.

Not really.

Wrecker, Pipe, Nickel, Maniac, Boink, Slayer, Brinks, and Freak were part of the Fallen Lords. Those were the people that Clash would be loyal to a fault to.

Not me.

"I know you're looking to move out of the clubhouse, and I want you to know whatever you need, I'll be there to help you."

I went numb and everything around me changed. I nodded and cleared my throat.

"Thanks. I'll remember that." I would remember a whole hell of a lot more than that. I would remember that everything I said to Clash could and would be repeated to Wrecker. "I actually need to run to the bathroom. Could you take these over to the table?"

Wrecker studied my face, but I must have been putting on a good face because he nodded his head and agreed. "Not a problem."

I plastered on a smile and made a quick detour over to my purse that was sitting on a table with all of the other girl's stuff.

Cora's keys were sitting next to my phone, and I grabbed both of them. I made my way to the bathroom, knowing I couldn't just run out the front door.

I spotted a side exit on the way to the bathroom, and I was out the door before I could really think about what I was feeling.

The key was in the ignition and my foot was on the gas pedal before I realized what I was doing.

I was running, and Clash wasn't coming with me.

*

Chapter Twenty-Two

Clash

Raven.

Beautiful. I need to you to call me.

Just text me to let me know you are okay.

I scrolled through all of the messages I had sent her the last four days, and she hadn't replied to one of them.

I had gone to the bathroom at the bowling alley. It seemed like the time was perfect for her and Wrecker to finally talk. Everything was good, and then suddenly, it wasn't.

No one knew why she ran.

She was there, and then, she was just gone.

For two days, I was convinced that someone had taken her, but the fact Cora's keys and her car were gone told us that Raven had taken the car again.

The only difference was this time, she wasn't answering my calls or texts.

We had searched every inch of Weston, and there wasn't a trace of her. It was like she had just disappeared into a cloud of smoke.

There was only one thing that was giving me hope.

The house she was buying was still under contract.

Her realtor didn't know where she was or what she was doing, but she did tell us that Raven had called to let her know she was going out of town, but she would be back in time for the closing on the house.

That was twenty-one days from now.

Three weeks and Raven would have to come back to Weston.

I wasn't going to stop looking for her until then, but I knew she wasn't going to make it easy for me to find her. Something had hurt her to make her run.

Wrecker was adamant about the fact that everything he and Raven had said was good. They hadn't argued, and she hadn't seemed like she was about to run.

He was as clueless as I was about the whole thing.

I looked around her room and sighed. Everything was still here except for her computer and some clothes. We had figured she must have made a quick pit stop at the clubhouse before leaving town.

She was gone right now, but I knew she would be back.

I just had to find a way to be patient and to not move heaven and earth to find her.

*

Chapter Twenty-Three

Raven

"Is there anything else I can get you, dear?"

I shook my head and handed her my debit card. "My waistline can only handle one croissant a day."

Lori smiled and swiped my card. "I think the table you like to sit at is open."

I grabbed my coffee and croissant. "Perfect. I've got a project I need to finish up before I head back home."

"Closing on the house already?" Lori handed my card back, and I tucked it in my pocket.

"Yeah. It's hard to believe that it's already been three weeks."

"Time flies when you're having fun." Lori winked.

I wouldn't go that far, but time sure did fly by. "I'm sure I'll be back up here for lunch later. Thanks, Lori."

I made my way over to the table by the window that I liked to sit at and set my computer, coffee, and croissant down.

For the past three weeks, I had been renting a room above the Sweet Bite bakery in Milfred Square and staying off the radar of the Fallen Lords. I had stolen Cora's car again, but she would have it back tomorrow when I signed the papers on my new house.

After that, I wouldn't be able to hide from the Fallen Lords anymore.

Clash texted me every day.

He called every day.

I had figured after a few days, he would just leave me alone but his calls and texts never stopped.

He wasn't as easy to shake as I thought he would be.

I was only an hour away from Weston, but it was far enough that no one ever came looking for me here.

Clash wasn't the only one who had called and texted me.

Wrecker called every day and left the same message. "*It's your brother. Call me so I know you are okay. Also, get your ass back home.*"

Every day the same and every day, I erased the message.

The only messages I didn't erase were the ones from Clash.

I was mad he had talked to Wrecker about me. The fact I was moving was mine to tell.

I was pissed that, once again, the MC was more important than me.

But none of that was enough to make me erase those messages.

There was so much going on in my head.

I should have told Clash that I didn't want him talking about me to anyone. Especially Wrecker. I had just taken the first step to moving past everything with Wrecker and then the fact Wrecker knew something about me he shouldn't have freaked the hell out of me. Did Clash tell him I was moving because he was supposed to be keeping an eye on me or had he just told a concerned brother that his sister was moving? I hadn't known the answer to that, but my instinct was to run.

I knew Clash couldn't read my mind, but to me, it seemed like common sense that I didn't want him telling my business to Wrecker.

My common sense obviously wasn't the same as others.

My phone buzzed, and I didn't have to look to know it was Clash texting me.

Morning, beautiful.

He still called me beautiful. He still texted me even though I had taken off without a word.

For a week, I had been pissed and justified my leaving by telling myself he had chosen the club over me.

Now I felt like a moron for running but didn't know how to fix it without looking like a psycho.

Tomorrow, I was going to have to face the music, and while I wasn't looking forward to it, I knew things would finally be ironed out tomorrow.

The messages Clash sent me suggested he would listen to me, but I didn't know if he would like what I had to say.

I was going to lay it all out and hoped to God he wouldn't run for the hills when I told him the Fallen Lords had no place in my life.

*

Chapter Twenty-Four

Clash

This swing was going to need some oil or something. It was squeaky as shit, and it was about to drive me fucking insane.

It was half past eleven, and I was sitting on Raven's porch swing waiting for her.

At first, I had thought about meeting her at the realtor's where she was supposed to sign the papers, but I didn't want to upset her and ruin the happy moment.

Instead, I was gonna ruin the moment she stepped foot in her new house.

"Fucking shit." I shot up from the swing and was about to leave when Cora's car pulled up to the curb and Raven stepped out.

She looked the same as she had three weeks ago.

Long black and red hair, svelte body, tattooed arms, and the small hoop in her nose shone in the sun.

She looked gorgeous.

"I was wondering when you were going to show up," she called. She reached into the back seat and grabbed a manila folder and her computer bag.

At least she was expecting me.

She walked up the sidewalk and stood at the bottom of the porch steps. I moved to the top step and looked at her.

"Would have showed up three weeks ago if you had told me where you went."

"Milfred Square."

My jaw dropped. "You happen to make it into Sweet Bite?"

"Uh, almost every day. They make a killer croissant."

I nodded. "Lori take your order?"

"Hold on. How the heck do you know about Sweet Bite *and* Lori?"

I laughed and shook my head. "'Cause I used to live there, and Lori is my mom."

"Oh, my God, " she gasped.

"Gotta admit, it is pretty surprising you wound up there."

Of all the places Raven could have gone, she wound up in the same town as my parents.

She fidgeted with the keys in her hand. "Just seemed like a good place to stop."

I shoved my hands in my pockets. "You think maybe we can talk?"

She bit her lip and nodded. "Yeah. I was gonna come find you if you didn't find me first."

She climbed the steps toward me, but I didn't move back when she was just a step down from me.

"I tried finding you, Raven. Everyday." I just never thought to check Milfred Square. I took a step back, and she stepped up the rest of the way.

"I didn't want to be found." She dropped the manila folder next to the front door and set her computer bag on top of it.

"Everything good to go with the house?"

She nodded and wiped her hands on her pants. "Yeah. Went smooth." She pulled a two keys out of her pocket and held them up. "It's all mine. Well, the house and a pretty big mortgage."

I sat down on the swing and patted the seat next to me.

She sat down, and we sat there swinging in silence.

"I don't really know where to start, Raven."

She turned sideways on the swing. "Then let me." She closed her eyes and took a deep breath. "I'm a bitch, Clash."

"No you're not, Ra—"

She put her hand up in my face. "Yes, I am. It's okay, Clash. I'm not stupid. I fully embrace the fact that I'm a bitch. It's just who I am." A smile spread across her lips. "Although I'd like to think I've been a nice bitch these past few weeks and I think I'll stick with that. I've got an attitude and just like you said, I had one hell of a chip on my shoulder." She sighed and closed her eyes. "And you had a huge part in helping me get over that. I'm not fully over my past, but you helped me understand that while it sucked back then, it's my past and that it shouldn't continue to define me."

"I said that?"

A light laugh escaped her lips. "No. You're really not that good with words, but I know that's what you were helping me to do."

"Then why did you run, Raven? I thought everything was going great and then you were gone."

"This is where I look like an idiot," she sighed.

I grabbed her hand and threaded my fingers through hers.

"You told my brother I had bought a house. Instead of running, I should have told you to keep your damn mouth shut when it comes to anything about me."

I pursed my lips. "Uh, no, I didn't."

She rolled her eyes. "Yes, you did, Clash. You don't have to lie to me."

"Raven. I haven't told anyone you were buying a house. Even right now, I'm the only one who knows this is yours."

She raised an eyebrow and pursed her lips. "But Wrecker told me he said I knew I was moving."

"Beautiful, I swear on my fucking Harley, I never told Wrecker you bought a house. I had just mentioned to him that you were looking at places but you weren't finding anything you liked. That was before you even put an offer in on this place."

She dropped her chin to her chest. "Oh, my God. I'm an even bigger idiot now."

"You thought I ran to Wrecker and told him your business, didn't you?"

She slowly raised her head and shrugged. "Maybe?" she drawled.

I threw my head back laughing. "Fucking hell, Raven. Why would I tell Wrecker your business? I now you have issues with him and I didn't want to cross the line when it came to him and you."

"I just thought that you told him because technically you're supposed to be keeping an eye on me and reporting back to Wrecker. In my head, you chose the club over me because you were telling Wrecker my business because that's what he wanted you to do."

"Jesus Christ, Raven. You think maybe you should have asked me what the hell was going on instead of running away? I haven't thought of you as a job for weeks. Even before that, when I did feel that way, I knew there had to be a hell of a lot going on with you for you to be acting the way you were."

"Clash, I suck at relationships," she whined. "I told you Mayra was the only friend I had and all I did was work. Besides, the only experience I've had with the club is the whole debacle with Wrecker choosing the club all of those years ago. He chose the club, and I figured you had just done the same thing."

"Did I at any time seem like I was choosing the club over you? Hell, Raven. I was the one who told Wrecker to go away when he was being a dick."

I thought she could see that. If I had been siding with Wrecker and reporting back to him with everything she was doing, she would have known that. Wrecker knew absolutely nothing about Raven while I was watching her. Boink had kept an eye on her when she first came to the clubhouse, but once Boink had shit going on with Mayra, Raven had become my responsibility.

She bit her lip. "I know," she muttered. "I just…it was easier to believe that you were just hanging around to report back to Wrecker than that you actually wanted to be with me. And, in my defense, I haven't had a good track record with people actually sticking around."

I pulled her into my lap and wrapped my arms around her waist. "Then I guess we're going to have to work on that."

She draped her arm across my shoulders and cradled my cheek with her hand. "I'm legit a hot mess, Clash. I'm still working on wrapping my head around everything that happened with Wrecker. I'm starting to see why he didn't fight for me, but I still have days where it hurts like it just happened."

"Raven, there's nothing wrong with feeling that way. It was a mistake that was made that set off a chain of shit for you. I think if you were completely fine and weren't upset about it, I would be more concerned."

Her fingers traveled over the stubble on my face, and she smiled.

"You can't smile like that and not expect me to kiss you, Raven. I've finally got you back in my arms and it's taking everything I've got not to lay you down in the backseat of Cora's car and have my way with you."

"What's stopping you from kissing me?" she whispered.

"Not a damn thing." I closed the gap between us and pressed my lips against hers.

It was a sweet kiss.

A kiss that held a shit-ton of promise and a hope for a future together.

"No one really knows I'm here?" she whispered against my lips.

I shook my head. "Not a soul. Wrecker has been going crazy looking for you, but I didn't tell him about the house. All I knew was you hadn't canceled the closing so I figured you would be back. Also, the fact I could see you were reading my messages."

"Yeah," she whispered. "Damn iPhone telling on me that I would read your messages as soon as you sent them."

I pressed a kiss to her lips. "That helped me, too"

"Though I am glad it doesn't show you how many times I listened to your voicemails and read your messages."

"Oh yeah?" I laughed. "You telling me that you missed me?"

She held up her finger and pointed finger an inch apart. "Maybe just a little."

"I missed you a hell of a lot more than that, beautiful."

"As you should," she sassed. "I am, after all, a prize idiot to have." She scurried off my lap and held the keys to the house in the air. "Now that we've figured that out and you know I'm an emotionally stunted fool, let's go check out my new house."

She stabbed the key in the door and swung the door open. Before she could step inside, I swung her up in into my arms. "Clash," she screeched. 'What are you doing?"

"Carrying you over the threshold." I walked into the house and turned in a full circle with her in my arms. "This place seems huge with no furniture in it."

"Speaking of that." Raven looked at her watch.

"Speaking of what, beautiful?"

A horn sounded outside, and huge smile spread across her lips. "The furniture is here."

"So while you were hiding in Milfred Square, you were giving your credit card a workout?" I laughed.

I set her feet on the floor but she held onto me and pressed another kiss to my lips. "I'm happy, Clash," she whispered.

"Good, beautiful. That's all I've ever wanted for you."

*

Chapter Twenty-Five

Raven

"Did you see her bed?" Mayra asked.

Karmen pointed at Mayra. "Yeah. I already told Nickel we seriously need an upgrade."

Nikki ran her hand over the arm of the couch. "I'm more in love with this couch. I don't even want to know how much you spent on this. It feels like butter under my butt."

"Butter? Under your butt?" Alice laughed. "I'm gonna have to talk to Pipe and ask just what you guys are doing. I might have to tell Wrecker to pick up some butter on the way home."

After Clash and I had directed the movers where all of the furniture belonged, Clash had sent Wrecker the address and told him to come over.

Now the whole club had invaded my house, and we had just finished eating the first meal in it.

None of the girls had demanded to know where I was or what had happened the past three weeks. It was like they didn't care what had happened as long as I was back.

"Ugh," Alice moaned. "I have the worst heartburn. I swear to God, this kid is going to come out with a full beard and Elvis hair."

Karmen choked on her beer, and Mayra smacked her on the back. "Keep it together, woman," Mayra giggled.

Karmen wiped her mouth with the back of her hand. "I just pictured a bearded Elvis coming out of your vajayjay."

Everyone busted up laughing.

"Oh, my God," Alice wailed. "I can't wipe that from my mind."

"Do I even want to know what hell you guys are laughing about?" Wrecker called through the screen door.

The guys had camped out on the porch, and the girls and I were sprawled out on my butter-like couch.

"We're just discussing what your baby is going to look like," Karmen wheezed. "You might want to invest in hair gel and beard conditioner."

"Fucking Christ," Wrecker grumbled.

Alice rubbed her stomach and looked at Wren. "Don't you have killer heartburn?"

Wren shook her head. "I'm great actually. I had a couple days of morning sickness but other than that, I don't even feel pregnant."

Alice groaned in disgust. "I hate you."

Karmen raised her hand to Alice. "I'm with you, Alice. When I was pregnant with Cole, I was absolutely miserable. It was a good thing I loved Nickel or I might have kicked his butt for getting me pregnant."

"You loved being pregnant," Nickel protested. "You're the one who keeps saying they want another one."

Karmen cradled Cole in her arms and pressed a kiss to his forehead. "How could you not want another one like him?"

"Every two hour feedings, leaky boobs, and no drinking for nine months," Nickel thundered.

Karmen squinted and wrinkled her nose. "Though I do think if you two have babies, there really isn't a reason for me to have another one."

Nickel laughed and leaned forward to look through the screen door. "Now remember that when you think you want another one."

Karmen stuck her tongue out at him. "I hate when you're right."

Nikki got up and stood at the screen door. "Now stop eavesdropping on our conversation or come in here so we don't have to scream."

The guys streamed back into the house and managed to cram themselves either on the couch or on the floor.

Wrecker nodded at me and walked into the kitchen.

"I'll be right back," I muttered to Clash. He pressed a kiss to the side of my head, and I followed Wrecker.

He was standing by the large sliding glass door looking into my backyard. "This place is nice, Raven."

"It is, isn't it?" I cleaned up the empty pizza boxes and set them next to the back door for me to take out to the garbage can later.

"You're doing good, Raven."

"Eh." I folded my arms over my chest and stood next to him. "It was touch and go there for a little bit."

He looked down at me. "But you made it through, Raven. No thanks to anyone but yourself."

I had made it through a lot. I was still dealing with some of it, but I was definitely on the other side of it now. "You would have been there if you would have known, Wrecker."

"You believe that or being a smartass?"

I laughed and bumped into him. "I believe it. But that doesn't mean it doesn't piss me off every now and then."

"You pissed off? Never," Wrecker chuckled. He sobered and stared into the backyard. "So this means you're sticking around for a while, right?"

"For a while," I mumbled.

"Good, good." He cleared his throat. "And you and Clash are good?"

I glanced up at him. "Is this you being the protective good brother?" I laughed.

He nodded.

"Clash and I are good, Wrecker. We got some stuff to work through too, but it's good."

Wrecker put his arm around my shoulders and pulled me into his side. "Good, brat. But just remember, if he pisses you off, I'm good at busting kneecaps and making it look like an accident."

*

Chapter Twenty-Six

Clash

"I don't know why the hell you are nervous."

Raven smoothed down her hair and glanced at me in the bathroom mirror. "Uh, because they're your parents."

"And you've already met my mom."

She fidgeted with her nose ring then bared her teeth in the mirror. "Is tea an in ma teth?"

"What in the world are you doing?" I laughed.

She closed her mouth and rubbed her lips together. "I asked you if there was anything in my teeth." She slathered some clear shit on her lips and turned to look at me. "What if your dad doesn't like my nose ring?"

"Why wouldn't he like it? It looks good." I squirted toothpaste on my toothbrush and ran it under the water.

"Because he's an engineer."

I glanced over at Raven. "You say that like it makes sense. He could be a fucking astronaut and he would be okay with your nose ring. My parents aren't judgy, Raven. You said yourself my mom loved you when you were at the bakery every day." I brushed my teeth and watched her fluff her hair then pat it down.

"She liked me when I was a stranger. Now I'm dating her son."

"We're dating?" I asked around a mouthful of spit.

"Aren't we?" she asked.

I shrugged and spit. "We live together so I guess we're dating."

Raven rolled her eyes and stormed out of the bathroom. "You're an idiot, Clash," she laughed.

I rinsed my mouth and turned off the water. "But I'm your idiot."

"That you are," she agreed. "We need to get going. The barbeque starts in half an hour, and we still need to load up all the crap I made."

I walked out of the bathroom and caught a glimpse of Raven's bare stomach while she changed her shirt for the fourth time. "Back to the first one?" I laughed.

She flipped me off and tugged the shirt down. "I'm trying to make a good impression."

She turned sideways and looked at herself in the mirror on the back of the bedroom door.

I pulled her into my arms. "You look beautiful. My dad will love your nose ring. My mom already loves you. The pasta salad tastes good. I ate six of the deviled eggs last night. Your hair looks amazing. Your ass looks amazing in these jeans."

She melted into my arms for a split-second but then smacked me on the shoulder. "I told you to stay out of the deviled eggs, Clash. Those are for the picnic, not your midnight snack," she scolded.

I tipped her head back and pressed a kiss to her lips. "They were good and you made eight dozen. It's safe to say you have enough and everyone is going to need a wide berth after eating that many eggs."

She wrinkled her nose and cringed. "Gross, Clash."

"Why do you think I used the downstairs bathroom this morning?"

"Oh, my God," she laughed. "I think this means the honeymoon stage is over for us."

"Nah." I delved my fingers in her hair. "Pretty sure it's always gonna be a honeymoon for us, beautiful."

She wagged her finger in my face. "Cut the sweet talk. We don't have time for it."

I kissed her quickly. "Then let's hit it."

"Maybe one more kiss wouldn't hurt," she whispered.

"There's my sweet girl."

One more kiss turned into us being ten minutes late to the picnic but it was totally worth it even though Raven bitched at me the whole way to the clubhouse.

*

Chapter Twenty-Seven

Raven

"They just pulled up."

I fanned my face with my hand and tried not to hyperventilate.

"Girl, what in the hell is wrong with you?" Alice laughed.

"I'm meeting Clash's parents and I actually want them to like me." I pulled on the hem of my shirt and fluffed my hair

Alice stuffed a deviled egg in her mouth and watched me fidget. "You look good. Not bitchy at all."

"She's right," Karmen agreed. "I think the pink makes you look approachable."

This was not helping my nerves at all.

Clash walked into the kitchen of the clubhouse and pulled me into his arms. "My parents are here, beautiful."

"Cool. I'll just go hide in the bathroom."

Clash held me tightly, and his body shook against mine.

"Can you please not laugh at me?"

"It's so hard not to." Clash leaned back and looked down at me. "You normally take no shit and don't give a fuck what people think."

"This is your parents," I stressed. "They're not just anyone."

He pressed a kiss to my lips. "And that's why I love you."

"No," I gasped. "No, no no. You do not get to tell me that right now. You do not get to do this to me right now, Clash."

Of course, Clash would pick just seconds before meeting his parents to tell me he loved me.

"Can't help it, beautiful. I love you." His eyes connected with mine, and I could see he meant each of those three words.

"I'm such a bitch, Clash," I cried. "You told me you loved me and I told you no."

Was I ever going to have the right response when something good happened?

"It's part of your charm, beautiful."

"And you're so nice to me even after I was a bitch. That makes me an even bigger bitch."

I was going to mess up this relationship before we really got started.

"I love you, Raven," he repeated.

I closed my eyes and sighed. "I love you too, Clash." My eyes popped open, and I realized I didn't even know Clash's real name. "I take that back. I want to say your real name the first time I tell you I love you."

"You can't take it back, Raven, but you can totally say it again." He leaned close and pressed his lips to my ear. "My name is Brent, beautiful."

Totally not what I expected it to be. "I love you, Brent," I whispered. I wrinkled my nose. "Okay, that's the only time I'm going to say that. You are definitely not a Brent."

He chuckled. "That's why I go by my road name."

"Okay," I sighed. I closed my eyes and took a deep breath. Everything was good, and it was only going to get better. I opened my eyes and looked at the man who loved me, bitchy attitude and all. "Let's go meet your parents."

*

Chapter Twenty-Eight

Clash

"She's pretty."

I glanced at my dad. "Mom?"

He chuckled. "Of course your mother, but I'm talking about Raven."

Raven and my mom were sitting around one of the picnic tables with all of the other ol' ladies. They didn't go thirty seconds without laughter erupting and Alice yelling she was gonna pee her pants if she laughed anymore.

"She's definitely easy on the eyes," I agreed.

"And you love her."

I nodded. "Yeah. She's the one, dad."

Dad patted me on the shoulder. "Then don't ever let her go, Brent."

I had no plans of ever letting Raven go.

She may be tough as nails and be a sarcastic smartass, but that really was all part of her charm. Raven was the perfect blend of sass, spitfire, and sweet.

A white sedan pulled into the clubhouse parking lot, and I looked over at Wrecker.

Everyone who we expected to show up for the picnic was here.

Wrecker warily watched the car, and I got an uneasy feeling in the pit of my stomach. Both the driver door and passenger door opened. Two women stepped out of the car.

Mayra jumped up from the picnic table she was sitting at. "Carnie? Wendy?"

Chapter Twenty-Nine

Carnie

I looked over the car at Wendy and gulped.

We had tried to avoid coming here, but Carnie and I had nowhere else to go.

Bobby was back, and he wanted me dead.

About the Author

Winter Travers is a devoted wife, mother, and aunt turned author who was born and raised in Wisconsin. After a brief stint in South Carolina following her heart to chase the man who is now her hubby, they retreated back up North to the changing seasons, and to the place they now call home.

Winter spends her days writing happily ever after's, and her nights with her hubby and son. She also has an addiction to anything MC related, her dog Thunder, and Mexican food! (Tamales!)

Winter loves to stay connected with her readers. Don't hesitate to reach out and contact her.

Facebook: www.facebook.com/wintertravers
Twitter: https://twitter.com/wintertravers
Instagram: https://www.instagram.com/wintertravers/
Website: www.wintertravers.com
Mailing List: http://eepurl.com/bYpIrD
Goodreads: https://bit.ly/2vAJPm1
BookBub: https://bit.ly/2HQtk7y
Pinterest: https://www.pinterest.com/wintertravers/

Coming Soon

May 9th

Mama Didn't Raise No Fool (I Ain't Your Mama Collaboration)

May 29th

Shutdown (Nitro Crew Series, Book 4)

July 29th

Freak (Fallen Lords MC, Book 7)

Check out the first chapter of Burndown

Burndown
Nitro Crew Series
Book 1

Chapter 1

Remy

"You need to call your mother."

"I talked to her last week."

Lo cleared his throat. "We are talking about the same woman, right?"

"The woman who treats me like I'm thirteen and not twenty-six." I sighed and dropped the wrench on the workbench.

"Okay, we're talking about the same woman. So, you should know you need to call her, because if you don't call her, then I have to deal with her, and while I love the hell out of your mother, I don't want to deal with her like that."

"I'm well aware of the ways you like to handle my mother." I shook my head, still trying to remove the image of what I had walked in on the last time I had been home. Thank God I had only seen Lo's ass and my mom's hand waving frantically. "You guys really shouldn't do that on the kitchen table. People eat there."

"And most people knock before they walk into someone's house."

I ducked out the side door of the shop and leaned against the brick wall. "This is what you called to talk to me about?"

"When did you become such an asshole?"

"Got that from you," I mumbled.

"Humph. You might wanna tone that down when you're talking to me. I could kick your ass."

"I always do enjoy these talks, Lo." He was an ass half of the time, but he was a good guy. Plus, he kept my mom happy, so I couldn't really find any fault with him.

His deep chuckle traveled through the phone. "Just call your mom when you get the chance. And by that, I mean call her today."

He disconnected the call before I could say any more. That was his way. He said what he needed to, and that was it.

"Don't you think you should be working on the car instead of gabbing on the phone?"

I shoved my phone into my pocket and twisted around to see Roc walking across the parking lot with a cup of coffee in his hand. From talking to one asshole to another.

"Just talking to Lo."

"Should I care who Lo is?" He stood in front of me with his hand in his pocket, looking like the asshole he was—ripped and tattered jeans, black boots, and a tight shirt stretched across his chest. I don't think I have ever seen him in anything other than what he was wearing today other than the color of the shirt varying. Today, he had on the same blue as the main sponsor for the Brooks Cummings Racing Team. Also known as the race team I was finally part of.

I shook my head. "Probably not. Just my mom's husband."

"Well, you can chit-chat on your own time. Right now, I need that new engine dropped into the car before five. We have time at the track tomorrow afternoon to see if it'll run well enough for the first race of the season." Roc nodded to the shop. "Once the engine is dropped, you can help with the clutch."

Roc wandered off around the building, leaving me stewing.

This was my dream job, but I fucking hated it because it wasn't *exactly* how I'd imagined my dream job. I was working for a top five NHRA team, but all I did was assist the clutch and driveline specialist. That was the job I really wanted. A specialist.

I needed to be grateful for the job I had since I was one of the youngest pit crew guys out there, but damn if I didn't want more. I could do the job. I just needed to put in my time and prove that I was here to stay.

"Get to work, Grain," Roc called.

Son of a bitch. That guy was on me like white on rice. I looked around but didn't even see Roc. How the hell did he know I was still standing here if I couldn't even see him?

"You need me to talk to him? Ask him to go easy on you?"

Fucking Frankie. "Still think you showed him your tits to get on his good side."

She stuck her head out the side door and laughed. "He's too old for me. I'm more into guys who couldn't pass for being my dad."

"That picky attitude is what's keeping you from finding a guy, Frank."

She shook her head. "Probably has to do with the fact people call me Frank, and I always have grease under my nails."

I grabbed the rag out of my back pocket and tossed it at her. "That'll help."

She rolled her eyes. "A dirty shop towel sure is going to fix all of my problems." She held open the door. "You helping me get the computer hooked up would actually help me more."

"You really think they are going to let me help you? Roc thinks the only thing I'm good for is standing over Ronald and handing him a wrench now and then." I hadn't been as lucky as Frankie. We had both gone through High Performance Engine Building in school, along with ten other courses that had prepared us to be on the Cummings Racing Team, but Frankie had stood out with her natural ability with computers and her eye for detail.

"If Roc wants to get out of here before nine, he won't mind you helping me."

I rolled my eyes and slid past her into the shop. "You can argue with him over me helping you." My eyes fell on Ronald, who was bent over the engine. "I'm sure ol' Ronald is almost done, anyway. He even thinks it's dumb for me to watch him."

Frankie clapped me on the shoulder. "Ronald is old. Ronald will not be doing this job two years from now. When Ronald races off into the sunset, you and I both know this job is as good as yours."

"Two years, Frank? I don't wanna have to wait that long to do a job I can do right now."

We watched Ronald slowly stand up from the engine with his hand on his back. "I'm thinking you might just have to wait one season." She laughed and headed to the other side of the garage.

"Grain, you wanna come over here? I want you to make sure I got those nuts on tight enough," Roland called.

I sighed and hung my head. This is what I was getting paid for—tightening nuts. Not like I was making some grand salary, but I had hoped to be doing more than this.

Patience.

The only problem with being patient was, I wasn't.

*

Grab your copy of <u>Burndown</u> today!

Printed in Great Britain
by Amazon